the fingertips of
DUNCAN DORFMAN

MEG WOLITZER

the fingertips of DUNCAN DORFMAN

DUTTON CHILDREN'S BOOKS
an imprint of Penguin Group (USA) Inc.

DUTTON CHILDREN'S BOOKS | A division of Penguin Young Readers Group
Published by the Penguin Group

Penguin Group (USA) Inc., 375 Hudson Street, New York, New York 10014, U.S.A. |
Penguin Group (Canada), 90 Eglinton Avenue East, Suite 700, Toronto, Ontario, Canada
M4P 2Y3 (a division of Pearson Penguin Canada Inc.) | Penguin Books Ltd, 80 Strand,
London WC2R 0RL, England | Penguin Ireland, 25 St Stephen's Green, Dublin 2, Ireland
(a division of Penguin Books Ltd) | Penguin Group (Australia), 250 Camberwell Road,
Camberwell, Victoria 3124, Australia (a division of Pearson Australia Group Pty Ltd) |
Penguin Books India Pvt Ltd, 11 Community Centre, Panchsheel Park, New Delhi—110
017, India | Penguin Group (NZ), 67 Apollo Drive, Rosedale, Auckland 0632, New Zealand
(a division of Pearson New Zealand Ltd.) | Penguin Books (South Africa) (Pty) Ltd, 24
Sturdee Avenue, Rosebank, Johannesburg 2196, South Africa | Penguin Books Ltd,
Registered Offices: 80 Strand, London WC2R 0RL, England

This book is a work of fiction. Names, characters, places, and incidents are either the
product of the author's imagination or are used fictitiously, and any resemblance to actual
persons, living or dead, business establishments, events, or locales is entirely coincidental.

The publisher does not have any control over and does not assume any responsibility for
author or third-party websites or their content.

SCRABBLE is a registered trademark of Hasbro, Inc. Neither the author nor the publisher
is associated with Hasbro, Inc., and Hasbro, Inc., has not authorized or endorsed the use
of the SCRABBLE name and any other intellectual property owned by Hasbro, Inc., on
or in connection with the publication of this book.

Library of Congress Cataloging-in-Publication Data

Wolitzer, Meg.
The fingertips of Duncan Dorfman / by Meg Wolitzer. — 1st ed.
p. cm.
Summary: Twelve-year-olds Duncan Dorfman, April Blunt, and Nate Saviano meet
at the Youth Scrabble Tournament where, although each has a different reason for
attending and for needing to win, they realize that something more important is at stake
than the grand prize.
ISBN 978-0-525-42304-1 (hardcover)
[1. Interpersonal relations—Fiction. 2. Individuality—Fiction. 3.Ability—Fiction.
4. Scrabble (Game)—Fiction. 5. Contests—Fiction.]
I. Title.
PZ7.W8338Fin 2011
[Fic]—dc22   2011005228

Published in the United States by Dutton Children's Books,
a division of Penguin Young Readers Group
345 Hudson Street, New York, New York 10014
www.penguin.com/youngreaders

DESIGNED BY IRENE VANDERVOORT | PRINTED IN USA | FIRST EDITION

2 4 6 8 10 9 7 5 3 1

For Charlie Panek—
formidable opponent, wonderful son

PART ONE

Chapter One
LUNCH MEAT AND THE CHINAMAN

On the night before his first day at his new school, in the small, squirrel-colored living room of his great-aunt's house, Duncan Dorfman's mother warned him not to show anyone his power. "Whatever you do, Duncan, keep it to yourself," she said. "If you don't, I'm afraid something bad will happen."

He had no idea why she was so worried. It wasn't as if people ever paid that much attention to him. In his last school, Duncan hadn't stood out in any way. He'd made a few friends, though no one who would particularly miss him now that he'd moved away. Besides, it wasn't as if the thing he could do was even useful.

"It's not a *power*," Duncan told his mother as they sat in the living room that night. She was laying out his clothes for school, which embarrassed him because he was twelve, not five. "A power," he said, "is when you can lift a car off a baby, or save the planet from destruction. That kind of thing."

"Then what would you call it?" his mother asked. She smoothed the creases on the ugly mustard-yellow shirt she had bought for him with her employee discount at Thriftee Mike's Warehouse.

"I don't know." What *did* you call the thing he could do? It didn't have a name. But he didn't want to upset her, so he promised that whatever the thing was, he would keep it to himself.

A week earlier, the two of them had gotten on a bus in Michigan with several suitcases and taped-up cartons, and then they had traveled for nine hours. At some point the bus stopped at a bad-smelling rest stop, and Duncan and his mother got out and bought French fries that seemed to have been cooked in oil left over from an ancient civilization. And then they got back on the bus and both of them gratefully closed their eyes, their heads knocking together occasionally in sleep.

Finally they arrived in Drilling Falls, Pennsylvania, the

town where Duncan's mother had grown up. There was nothing exciting about Drilling Falls, and she had said she didn't have many happy memories of growing up there, but they had nowhere else to go. She had lost her job as the manager of a gift shop in Michigan, and when his great-aunt heard this, she had invited them to come live with her.

Aunt Djuna was a box-shaped old woman who wore a green sweater over her shoulders, and who, as she liked to tell people, never ate anything with a face. You would walk into her front hall and a yam or bean aroma would hit you, the same way that the smell of brownie mix or roast chicken would float your way in other houses.

His mother often said, "We should be very grateful to Aunt Djuna. We should kiss the ground she walks on. She gave us a home, and found me a job."

Thanks to Aunt Djuna, Duncan's mother now worked at Thriftee Mike's Warehouse, a superstore with bins of random items like double-A batteries and pig-shaped staplers. Though very few people had spent any time with Thriftee Mike himself, he was a real, thirty-year-old man named Michael Scobee, who lived in the rich section of Drilling Falls. Duncan had heard him described as an eccentric millionaire who wore high-top sneakers and ate junky cocoa-and-marshmallow-flavored cereal for breakfast. No one really knew much else about him, because he only came to the store once in a while, very late at night, when no one was there except the security guards. He wasn't supposed to be "good with people," and so he stayed away during the day.

"That's fine with me," Duncan's mother had said. "I don't need to see him."

The employees at Thriftee Mike's wore red smocks with name tags that read, I'M THRIFTEE SUE or, I'M THRIFTEE PETE. Or, in Duncan's mother's case, I'M THRIFTEE CAROLINE. Caroline Dorfman was a nice person, pretty, blond-haired, and funny, but she worried all the time—mostly about Duncan. She'd raised him all by herself, because his father Joe Wright had died of a rare disease called panosis before Duncan was born.

"It was very sad," she would say quietly, but she didn't like to say too much else about it. All Duncan knew was that his parents had been young when he was born, and that they hadn't been married. That was about the extent of his knowledge.

Duncan's mother got migraine headaches when she was under stress. Usually, right before the headache came on, her vision would be clouded with a silvery light she called an aura. The next thing Duncan knew, she would say, "Oh no, another aura. I'm sorry, Duncan, I'll see you later, honey, okay? Make yourself a PB&J for lunch. And we have plums!" Then she'd go into her bedroom and lie in the dark until the migraine passed. Over the years, Duncan had brought up the subject of his father less and less often, because he knew it really upset her.

Just like now, when she asked Duncan not to show anyone his so-called power, he knew he should do what she wanted, or else she might get agitated. The only reason Duncan had shown it to her in the first place was that it had taken him by surprise. He had been in his new bedroom two days earlier, sitting on the bed flipping through an old book—something dumb about a kid named Jimmy who builds a rocket ship with his best friend, a gopher—when suddenly Duncan discovered that he could do the strangest thing.

It had shocked him, so he'd gone out into the hallway, where his mother was unpacking boxes from the move, and he'd said to her, "Mom, check this out."

That was his first mistake.

She'd looked up, distracted, smiling, a mermaid lamp in one hand. He'd showed it to her, and in her astonishment she dropped the lamp to the floor, cracking off a piece of the mermaid's tail. "Oh my God, Duncan," she'd finally whispered, "you have a *power*."

"No I don't," he said. Duncan Dorfman wasn't that kind of person. He wasn't powerful in any way at all. He thought of himself as ordinary—*less* than ordinary. He was a little thick-chested, wavy-haired, and, these days, nerd-shirted. He wasn't good at sports or science. He couldn't tell a joke well. He didn't know everything about every dinosaur that ever existed, or every rock. He didn't have any passions, let alone any powers.

"Well, I think you do," she insisted. "And it's the kind of thing that could get attention. That's the last thing we need while we're starting from scratch here in my old town. Please don't show it to anyone else, okay, honey?"

"Okay," Duncan said, though her fear didn't make sense to him.

"*No one,*" said his mother.

"What shouldn't Duncan show anyone?" Aunt Djuna asked as she came into the hallway with an armful of root vegetables that poked out like the snouts of strange little animals.

"Oh, nothing, Djuna," said his mother, shooting him a keep-quiet look.

There were other secrets in this house, too, Duncan thought. Just the night before, when he was lying in bed, he had heard his mother and Aunt Djuna whispering together in the living room. As he fell asleep, he'd heard fragments of what they were saying:

"*. . . I realize it's not perfect,*" his mother said.

And his great-aunt said, "*He deserves better . . .*"

"*I know, I know,*" said his mother.

In the morning at breakfast, when Duncan asked her

what they had been talking about—what wasn't perfect, and who deserved better—she said she couldn't remember. "I'm sure it wasn't anything important," she said, and he let it drop.

And now here they were, at nine P.M. on the night before school was to begin, and secrecy was in the air again.

"Remember, keep it to yourself," his mother said, handing him his stiff yellow shirt and green pants. From across the room, Aunt Djuna, now fast asleep in the big old recliner, made quiet yipping sounds. It was almost bedtime, and Duncan promised his mother again that he wouldn't tell anyone.

Duncan tried. He seriously did. But sometimes your talent—your tiny, weird skill, or even your power—just has to get out.

For five more weeks, though, it stayed in. Not only that, but he almost forgot about it. During that time, Duncan Dorfman became just one of three hundred seventh graders in the Drilling Falls Middle School. Every morning, he walked through the halls in the overflowing crowd of kids, floating along like a leaf carried on a breeze. Then, after thumping his heavy backpack into locker #299, he headed for class. No one knew him, and no one cared.

And even though, that first day, the homeroom teacher

had said to the class, "Listen up, people! Be sure to include our new students at lunchtime!" no one did.

There was another new kid that fall; his name was Andrew Tanizaki, and he had a face like a tired old man. People sometimes called Andrew the "Chinaman," despite the fact that his grandparents were originally from Japan, and that Andrew and his parents were from New Jersey. Duncan Dorfman and Andrew Tanizaki sat together every day at lunch. No one else came to sit with them. It was just them, Duncan and the Chinaman, sitting across from each other in the cafeteria at 10:45 A.M. with their damp red trays.

If only Duncan liked Andrew Tanizaki more! But this was what the conversation between them at the lunch table was like:

Andrew: Do you play the video game Starpod Defenders: Team Zero?

Duncan: No.

Andrew: Well, I do, and I beat level twelve. Only two other players in North America have done that. One is five years old. The other one has no hands. He was born that way, you know. Handless.

Duncan: Oh.

Then there was an awkward silence, except for the chewing of food. The chewing went on and on.

One day, after they sat uncomfortably like this for a while, Duncan finally stood up to get himself a glass of apple juice, and as he walked across the cafeteria he felt something go *slap* against his back. He reached around, but didn't feel anything, so he just got his juice and walked back to his seat. There was distant laughter, and the sounds of people shouting something, but Duncan paid no attention. As he reached his table, though, the shouting became harder to ignore.

"LUNCH MEAT!" people were calling out. "HEY, LUNCH MEAT!"

After a few seconds, Duncan Dorfman realized they were talking to *him*.

He stood still, his face growing pink, but he had no idea of why they were saying this, or what it meant. It was as if the kids at this school shouted strange, random words at new kids in order to freak them out. Maybe in previous years they had shouted at other new kids, "HEY, BLOWFISH!" or, "HEY, MONKEY WRENCH!"

But then Andrew Tanizaki stood up and hurried over to Duncan. "Uh, Duncan? You have lunch meat on your back," he whispered.

"What?"

"Lunch meat."

Duncan reached around himself again, feeling all over the places on his back that he could reach. This time, his hand found the edge of something cold and damp, and he pulled it off slowly and fearfully, as if taking off a Band-Aid.

Someone had flung a piece of baloney at his back, and it had just stayed there, sticking to his yellow shirt. And now, like Andrew Tanizaki, aka the Chinaman, Duncan Dorfman had a nickname, too: Lunch Meat.

Just as the lunch meat had stuck to his shirt, the name stuck to Duncan.

"Yo, Lunch Meat!" kids said to him every day at school. Even a sixth-grade girl who had seemed to be a nice person called him that one day, her face formed into a sneer.

After a few days, kids stopped calling out to Duncan as much; they seemed to lose interest in this new boy who was becoming not so new anymore. But still the name was there; he had been branded Lunch Meat. He eventually returned to his grim routine of mostly being ignored, except once in a while when someone called out the nickname for no particular reason.

Life was joyless—that was the best word for it. Duncan slogged through the days, and at night he couldn't wait to go to sleep. He would lie in bed and listen to his mother and his great-aunt have one of their whispery conversations about whatever private thing it was they talked about when he wasn't around, and then he would finally fall asleep. It might have gone on and on like this all year.

But inside him, it was all getting to be too much.

On a cold, slushy morning in October, five weeks after school began, sleet was *pinging* the windows outside the cafeteria, and someone across the room was calling out, "Hey, Lunch Meat!" and Andrew Tanizaki's jaw was biting down squeakily on a hot dog. All of it—the depressing weather, the nickname, the sounds, the loneliness—finally became unbearable.

Duncan wondered if there was a way out. He could get on a bus and go somewhere . . . but where? He had no money. He had no father. He had no one and nothing other than a nice but overprotective, migraine-getting mother who worked long hours at Thriftee Mike's. He thought about how much she had wanted him to hide his special ability from everyone.

That was when it hit him.

In order to have a decent future at Drilling Falls Middle School, he had to ignore what she wanted. *Sorry, Mom,* he said to himself. And then he sat up a little straighter and told Andrew Tanizaki, "I have a power."

The words were forbidden, but it was almost as if he hadn't said anything at all. Andrew barely looked up from his food. "Yeah, right," he finally said.

"I do."

Andrew took his pinky finger and reached deep into his own mouth, trying to loosen a tiny piece of hot-dog skin from between the tight clamps of his braces. Then he folded his arms across his chest and said to Duncan Dorfman, "Show me."

Chapter Two

THE SO-CALLED POWER IS REVEALED

Give me something to read," Duncan told Andrew.

"Why, am I boring you?"

"I don't mean to read to *myself*," said Duncan. "Something I can read out loud."

"I already know you can read," said Andrew Tanizaki. "You don't have to prove it to me."

"Tanizaki, just give me something, okay?" Duncan said impatiently.

Andrew reached into the clogged backpack he took everywhere and pulled out a creased little booklet. It was a Starpod Defenders instruction manual; Andrew had doodled cartoons all over it. Pictures of alien heads floated everywhere, all of them with long antennae coming out of their straight black hair.

"Now open to a random page," said Duncan.

"There's no such thing as random," Andrew said. "My brother says—"

"Do you want me to do this or not?"

Without waiting for an answer, Duncan closed his eyes and turned his head away as Andrew opened the booklet and slid it toward him.

"Okay," said Andrew. "Here."

There was silence, or at least there was silence at their end of the table. All around them, kids talked and shouted and laughed. The seven-foot-tall cafeteria giantess blew on a whistle, then Duncan heard her yell, "IF YOU DO NOT SIT DOWN, YOUNG LADY, YOU WILL HAVE LUNCH WITH PRINCIPAL GLOAM!"

After a second, Duncan realized that the sounds of the whistle and the voices were fading. It was as if he and Tanizaki were on a train carrying them far away from Drilling Falls Middle School. Duncan felt the fingertips of his left hand grow warm, then warmer, then actually *hot*, as if he had one of those hand warmers in his pocket that his mother used to buy him.

Now, just the way it had happened in the bedroom with the dumb book about Jimmy and the gopher and the rocket ship, the fingers of his left hand became hotter and hotter. It was as though his brain was sending his fingers an urgent message: MUST—HAVE—HEAT. They grew so hot they began to hurt, and soon they *pulsed* as though someone had slammed a car door on them. When it seemed as though he couldn't stand the heat any longer, it leveled off, and Duncan let out his breath in relief.

"Are you okay?" he heard Andrew Tanizaki say, and Duncan just nodded. With his eyes still shut, he ran the fingertips of his left hand across the surface of the open booklet and read aloud:

"FAQ's.

Question 1: What happens if I reach a new level and get stuck inside the Mindvault?

Answer: If you reach one of the master levels, you should feel proud! But for those who are really impatient, cheats for reaching the next level can be found inside the Conestar Satellite."

Duncan paused. "And I also want to add, Andrew," he said, "that you drew some doodles. They're pretty good, too. They're these little cartoons of aliens trapped in what I think is supposed to be the Mindvault. Am I right?"

There was no reply. Duncan stopped talking and opened his eyes. The world seemed as bright as Thriftee Mike's, and the sounds of the cafeteria rolled back toward him.

He turned to face Andrew, who was just staring at him,

and who then muttered in a shocked voice, "Yeah, you're right. What the heck *is* this, Dorfman?"

Duncan Dorfman hadn't let his power out in order to impress Andrew Tanizaki. Impressing him wouldn't improve Duncan's loneliness or nothingness at school. He had done it because he knew that if something unusual happened at their cafeteria table, the kids at the next table would know about it, too.

So after Duncan Dorfman read the instruction manual from Starpod Defenders aloud without looking at the words, he wasn't surprised to see a boy across the way glance over.

Carl Slater was a smirking kid with a rust-colored buzz cut that always looked freshly mowed. He sat in the cafeteria at the next table every day with a bunch of other kids, playing Scrabble®. They were all members of the Drilling Falls Middle School Scrabble Club, though anyone who saw the way they behaved might have thought they were looking for trouble rather than a friendly game. The year before, Carl Slater had gotten into trouble so many times at school—he'd talked back to his English teacher; he'd accepted a dare to steal the notebook of a girl named Ariel Berk; he'd stood behind the cafeteria giantess and walked with his arms stretched out like Frankenstein's monster— that the principal, Mr. Gloam, had insisted that he join a club and devote himself to it.

"Do something useful with yourself, Mr. Slater, or you will be suspended," said Mr. Gloam. "Simple as that."

The principal said it couldn't be a sport. He wanted Carl to focus on using only his brain for a change. The Scrabble Club, at that point, was very small: basically two kids in a room with an old board. It was Carl's mother's idea that he join the Scrabble Club. She thought it would help him get into college someday.

On the first day, Carl had to be dragged in. But soon he found that he was surprisingly good at Scrabble, and then he convinced his friends to join, too. Because they always did what Carl Slater said, the Scrabble Club was quickly filled with loudmouthed kids, slightly wild kids, kids like Carl Slater. And they all got pretty good at the game and began to compete in local tournaments against other schools' Scrabble Clubs.

The year before, Drilling Falls Middle had sent Carl Slater and Brian Kalb off to the YST—the Youth Scrabble Tournament—which was held down in Yakamee, Florida, every December. They'd had a good time, and placed forty-sixth out of one hundred teams. Carl and Brian had returned home with a small trophy showing what appeared to be a gold-plated pizza deliveryman holding up a pizza box—but was really a person holding up a giant Scrabble tile.

The first-place winners of the tournament had taken home *ten thousand dollars*, Duncan had heard someone at school say. If Duncan had ten thousand dollars—or half of it, anyway (kids' tournament Scrabble was usually played in teams of two)—he would give it to his mother, and maybe they could rent their own place.

Carl Slater liked to tell people that the letters in his last name could be moved around to spell ten different words, both ones that were ordinary, and ones that weren't. These included:

ALERTS
ALTERS
ARTELS
ESTRAL
LASTER
RATELS
SALTER
STALER
STELAR
TALERS

All of which, Carl explained to anyone who would listen, were words you could play in a game of Scrabble. Carl was both popular and mean, smart in the way that an animal in an Aesop's fable is smart. He was a good athlete, too, but lately he'd become much more obsessed with Scrabble than sports. If Duncan hadn't shown Andrew Tanizaki his power, then Carl Slater would never have seen it; but Carl, of course, saw everything. When he noticed something peculiar going on at the lunch table across from the one where he usually sat, he needed to find out more.

Now he squinted at Duncan in the cafeteria, finished his lunch, then stood up and walked over, sitting on the bench beside Tanizaki and directly across from Duncan.

Carl's friend Mitchell Farley called, "Yo, Carl, what are you doing?"

"Busy," said Carl, waving him off.

"BUSY is an anagram of YUBS," said Mitchell. He was always looking for a way to improve his Scrabble skills.

Carl just looked at him. "YUBS isn't a word, Farleyface," he said coldly. "But BUYS is. BUYS is an anagram of BUSY."

"Oh. Right," said Mitchell.

Carl Slater turned to Duncan and said, "Hey, Lunch Meat, what were you and the Chinaman just doing?"

"Nothing," said Duncan.

"Some kind of sad, sad magic trick that you found inside a cereal box?" asked Carl.

"No," said Duncan. "It wasn't a trick."

"Seriously, Dwarfman," said Carl, "I saw what you were doing. You, like, you *memorized* the Chinaman's video-game booklet."

"I didn't memorize it. Tell him, Tanizaki."

"Um, Duncan?" piped up Andrew in a nervous voice, and he stood up. "I just remembered I have to go see the nurse about that nosebleed I had last week—"

"WHY ARE YOU STANDING UP?" cried the cafeteria giantess, casting her long shadow across the table. "SIT DOWN, OR YOU'LL BE EATING WITH PRINCIPAL GLOAM!" she said, and Tanizaki shrank back down. Her shadow lurched elsewhere.

"I read the words with my fingers, not my eyes," Duncan said. "It's this thing I can do."

"So, like, you're telling me you can *feel the words* underneath your fingers?" said Carl Slater, not taking his eyes off Duncan.

Duncan nodded, trying to appear calm. "Yeah. But only the left hand. The right hand doesn't work." Then he added, "And I can feel pictures, too."

From across the table, Andrew Tanizaki watched with quivering, hamsterish excitement. By now, everyone else who'd been sitting at the Scrabble table had come over, and a few people from other tables came over to see what was going on, too. Someone took out a blindfold and wrapped it around Duncan Dorfman's head, tying it with a sharp jerk. It was really a pair of gym shorts; Duncan could smell the big, stinking gym beneath the slippery fabric. He smelled a thousand long-ago dodgeball games, and he imagined himself getting smacked in the head and the stomach with ball after ball.

Someone else put a magazine under his hand and said in a nasty voice, "Read, Lunch Meat."

The table became quiet. If Duncan was ever going to have a chance to rise up from his loneliness and his loserdom and the fact that he was just Lunch Meat—a boy who was forced to sit with the Chinaman, a boy who was stuck here in Drilling Falls in a peculiar-smelling little house with his mother and his great-aunt—then this was the moment.

This was it.

Though his mother desperately didn't want him to stand out, he knew what he had to do. No one in this school imagined that Duncan Dorfman had anything special to offer. But maybe they were wrong, Duncan thought, and he felt his fingertips crackle once again with heat. He made his voice get loud as he said, "Road Rage Magazine. *Inside: Hot wheels and hot babes—we've got 'em!*"

The kids around the table started to laugh; someone clapped. It wasn't just Duncan's fingers that burned; his face did, too. He couldn't help but show off a little as he sat in the *good* kind of spotlight for the first time in his life, and so he added, "Then there's a picture of a guy driving a sports car. And a woman in a bikini is lying on the hood, drinking . . . a glass of lemonade, I think. At least, there's a slice of lemon on the side of the glass."

"He's seen it before!" someone insisted.

Someone else said, "He's memorized it! He's got, like, one of them photogenic memories!"

A third person yelled, "What a big dumb fake! Fakey McFakester!"

A book was angrily shoved at Duncan, so he began to read it aloud, despite having gym shorts on his head. He read, *"Was Christopher Columbus really the hero that people say he was?"*

The kids around the table howled; it was like lunchtime at a school for wolves. Duncan Dorfman was handed math books; diagrams of spores; sheet music from the school's a cappella group, the Drilltones. He quickly went from being unknown to being surrounded.

"I have plans for you, Lunch Meat—I mean, Dorfman," whispered Carl Slater. "You ever hear of the YST? The Youth Scrabble Tournament?"

"Yeah," said Duncan.

"Well, it's coming up on December twelfth."

"I don't really play Scrabble."

"With your skill, you could be in it this year. You get what I'm saying?"

"No," said Duncan.

"Think about it, Dorfman. You could pick letters from the bag like they were cherries from a tree," said Carl. "The tiles used in tournaments are called Protiles, and they aren't engraved with letters; they're just stamped in ink. There's no way to tell what letters they are when they're in the bag.

There's no way for a *normal* person to tell, I mean. But you could do it. You're not normal. You're a *freak*, Dorfman. But in a good way," he added quickly.

"Is it legal?" Duncan asked doubtfully.

"No, Dorfman, you'll probably be arrested. The cops will put you in handcuffs and you'll be sent to death row." Carl paused, sighing. "Is it legal? *Of course it's legal!* Jeez! The rules of Scrabble don't say anything about some freaky fingertip power. Think of the glory, Dorfman. Think of the *cash*." He paused. "I hear that you and your mom have no money, am I right?" Duncan didn't say anything. "I hear that your dad died of some disease," said Carl.

"Panosis," said Duncan.

"Whatever. And that you and your mom live in some cousin's house for free, because she feels sorry for you—"

"Great-aunt."

"Fine! Great-aunt! And that your mom works at Thriftee Mike's, and that your life is a little grim." Duncan felt his shoulders tense up, and he opened his mouth, but Carl said, "Relax, Dorfman. I'm not mocking you. I'm just saying this doesn't have to be the case anymore. We'll talk later at your locker, okay?"

"Okay," said Duncan, but he felt deeply uncomfortable, and almost about to throw up, or faint and fall down on the floor.

Carl Slater left the table just as Duncan was carried off into the sea of kids. Somewhere in that sea, Andrew Tanizaki's head bobbed up, then went under. It would be a long time before the two of them would sit at the same lunch table again.

Chapter Three

A FISH OUT OF WATER
IN A FAMILY OF JOCKS

All the way across the country in Portland, Oregon, April Blunt sat in her bedroom making flash cards. Her hand wrote out card after card about photosynthesis, but her mind was focused not on plants, but on a person. She didn't know his name, his e-mail address, his phone number, where he lived, or anything else. They had met once at a motel pool when she was nine, and had spent a couple of hours together. He was a mystery to her, but still she'd been thinking about him off and on for all this time.

The boy was the first person who had ever been

impressed by her Scrabble skills. But it wasn't just that. He'd also made it clear in their brief time together that he liked hanging around April when she talked about Scrabble. She didn't bore him. Looking back, she realized that he was the first person who'd let her feel like the best version of herself. Later on, other people did that, too, including Lucy Woolery, who became her closest friend and Scrabble partner. But he was the first one, and she thought about him often.

"I'll tell you one thing," she said to Lucy, who was sitting at the foot of April's bed, making her own far neater flash cards. "The boy I met back then was a lot more interesting to me than photosynthesis."

"I like photosynthesis," said Lucy. "It's plants *breathing*, basically. How sick is that? But of course he was more interesting. Especially since you don't know who he is or what happened to him."

A vague picture of the boy who April had met at the motel pool was vacuum-packed inside her brain forever. She and this boy had had a great time during the couple of hours they had spent together. They had talked a lot, and she'd taught him to play Scrabble, and then it was over, *bam*.

"It's amazing that you still think about him," said Lucy. "Can't you find out where he is?"

"You can't look someone up if you don't know their name," said April.

"Yes, you can," said Lucy. "My parents do it all the time."

"What do you mean?"

"We'll be at dinner, and my mom will say, 'Paul, who was that actor? The one with the scar on his lip who was in that movie about the deranged zookeeper?' Then they'll send me off to get my laptop, and I'll type in 'actor,' 'scar,' 'lip,' and 'zookeeper.' And up pops the name."

"But this is different," said April. "I can't just search for this kid under 'Boy Who I Met at a Motel Pool Three Years Ago and Who Liked Listening to Me Drone on About Scrabble and Who I Never, Ever Saw Again.'"

"That's true," Lucy said.

"If I don't know this boy's name, I can't get any information. It's just one of those things." April paused. "You meet somebody, and then your parents say, 'Okay, great, I'm glad you've been having fun. But now it's time for us to go.' And because you're a minor, you have to leave with them, and you and the other person never see each other again. It's actually kind of sad the way kids have no control over their own lives. We're just basically . . . puppets being ordered around by cruel puppeteers."

"Yeah," said Lucy. "It's totally tragic. The tragedy of the tormented, underage puppets."

April took a pillow and thumped it down on Lucy, who laughed hard as some small, curling feathers swooped through the air.

The house was quiet on this clear October Saturday, though out in the backyard there was shouting as usual. "Hut one, hut two, hut three, HIKE," someone cried, and everyone in the family moved their solid, sporty bodies across the crunching grass.

The Blunts were a family of jocks. All of them had thick, strong necks, except for April, who had always seemed different. The three other Blunt children had weighed over nine pounds at birth and had had broad shoulders, full heads of hair like carpeting, and mashed faces that already gave them the appearance of being jocks.

April was born weighing four pounds, eleven ounces. She didn't have a single hair on her head. "You were like a little goldfish," her father sometimes said. If he hadn't actually witnessed the moment she popped out into the world, he would have sworn that they had been given the wrong baby.

But April *was* a Blunt. As she got older, she still looked nothing like them (she was small, with red hair and nearly see-through pale skin), and acted nothing like them, either, but she *was* one of them—the one who did not "get with the program," as she often said to her best friend.

Lucy Woolery always nodded and said, "That must be hard," though she couldn't relate. The Woolerys were all alike: three tall, skinny, incredibly organized people who were good at everything and had skin of an identical deep brown.

The Blunts had put April through a series of secret tests over time, as if to reassure themselves that she was one of them. She had failed every test. They gave her the first one when she was eighteen months old, handing her a soccer ball and saying, "Here you go! A ball! A ball for April!"

She held it in her hands, stuck out her tongue and licked it, and put it down. Then she waddled over to the refrigerator door and moved the magnetic alphabet letters around in a big swirl until they spelled the word BALL.

"Oh my God," said her mother.

"Unbelievable," said her father.

They turned to each other and whispered in frantic voices. Her parents had both been shocked at her verbal skills, but disappointed that she hadn't given the ball a good hard kick or, better yet, a slamming head-butt.

There were other tests later on that involved memorizing the names of team cheers. At this she was also hopeless. "Go . . . Rainers?" she would chant with doubt in her voice.

"It's Raiders, not Rainers," her parents said. "Try it again."

When April was six years old she started playing Scrabble, and right away it was obvious that she was good at it. She read word lists, and taught herself the two-letter words that were acceptable in Scrabble—words like XI and PE and HM, and also a few new ones, including QI and ZA.

April still didn't know what many of these words meant, but she knew that ZA was short for *PIZZA*, even though no one ever said, "Mmm, I'm starving! I wish I had a nice, piping hot slice of pepperoni *za*."

Whoever came up with the words that were acceptable in the Scrabble dictionary seemed to have a warped view of life, April thought. Why was ZA good, but, say, GA wasn't? More babies probably said GA than all the people combined who called pizza ZA, but those were the rules.

April had first gotten to know Lucy Woolery a year earlier, in sixth grade, after the Woolerys had moved here from another town in Oregon. She soon learned that Lucy was a talkative and interesting girl who played Scrabble, too. Other kids would say, "Oh, I like Scrabble a lot," but when April actually sat down to play them, they did something like try to make words on a diagonal, or insisted that something like FLINK was a word.

"Are you thinking of FLUNK?" April had politely asked a boy.

"Nope. FLINK," he'd said, and then she'd challenged him, and the word had had to be removed from the board.

A few days later, a girl played CURNISH, and April kindly said, "Are you thinking of FURNISH? Because

CURNISH isn't a word." She offered the girl a chance to take back her word without a penalty.

But the girl said, "It is too a word. It's a kind of tree." So April had challenged her, and that word had had to be taken off, too.

April didn't need other players to be really good, but it was more entertaining when they knew the basics. Lucy did, and they became great friends and opponents. There were never hard feelings when one of them crushed the other. They always shook hands across the board at the end, and went to do something else. Occasionally April and Lucy referred to each other by the names Flink and Curnish. Someday, Lucy said, they would become lawyers and open a practice together called Flink & Curnish, Limited.

"Why do they always say 'Limited'?" April asked, but Lucy had no idea.

The two of them talked about everything. "Have you ever noticed," Lucy asked recently as they sat in her room with her dog, Bear, sleeping on the floor between them, "that dogs smell like corn chips?"

"No," April said. But Lucy was right. Dogs—their paws in particular—did smell like corn chips: slightly salty, with a good, tangy, fried odor. Lucy was always right.

Another time, when they were walking home from school in the fall and kept stopping to step on particularly crunchy-looking leaves, Lucy asked, "How come humans love the sound of leaves crunching? We go out of our way to hear it, to feel it. Why is it so insanely satisfying?"

April said she had no idea. But of course it was a good question.

The girls played Scrabble all the time in their middle school. Lucy was good at everything: sports, English, math, science, drawing, and Scrabble. On December twelfth, they would be playing as a team at the Youth Scrabble Tournament in Yakamee, Florida. Though April's parents had agreed that she could go, they had no interest in anything as unsporty as Scrabble.

Lately, April had had a persistent fantasy: if she and Lucy made it to the final round of the YST, her family would finally respect her. She had read online that the finals would be broadcast live on the cable sports channel *Thwap!* TV. If she and Lucy appeared on that channel, her family would realize that Scrabble *was* a sport. It was a sport of the brain.

Sometimes April dreamed about sports. Occasionally in the dreams she was actually playing, wedged in the middle of a family scrimmage in a football stadium. Yet at the very last minute, when everyone was counting on her to make the winning field goal, she would freeze.

"You can do it!" one of her sisters would shout.

"Come on, April, you're one of us!" cried her brother. "Do it for the Blunts!"

"Do it for me," someone else said quietly, and in the

dream she always turned sharply toward the voice in the stands.

"*It's you,*" she would say in amazement. "The boy from the motel pool. *Where are you*?" she would whisper.

But right before she was about to find out, April always woke up.

Chapter Four
ROAST MULES

The dreams had started three years earlier, the night after April met the boy. The Blunt family had been on the road; her siblings were playing in travel baseball and softball games that weekend, and so her parents had decided that the family would spend the night at some motel. The one they chose wasn't very busy, and had a swimming pool. The Blunts went to sleep not too long after dinner, for they were planning to get up early in the morning. April had gotten permission to spend the next day at the motel by herself.

It was ten A.M. by the time she woke up, and everyone was already gone. April got dressed and went outside onto the second-floor landing. She could see into the fenced-in pool area, where a boy about her age was standing in bathing trunks and a T-shirt, looking down into the water. April changed into a bathing suit, too, and soon she was at the pool, sitting on a lounge chair with her travel Scrabble set open in her lap. She often played against herself, drawing two separate racks of tiles. When she traveled with her family, there was no other choice.

The boy paced the edge of the pool. If he'd been in April's family, he would have already been in the water, doing cannonballs and shouting, "Look at me, everybody!" But he seemed reluctant. April got up and dipped in a foot.

"It's warm," she announced.

"I figured," said the boy. He was thin, with a nice face, and a blue T-shirt that had some words printed on it in white.

"Don't you swim?" she asked him.

"I used to. But then I found out I have serious food allergies."

"You can't swim because of allergies?" April asked.

"Well, I got kind of skinny when they were trying to figure out what I was allowed to eat. So I don't like to take my shirt off. I look too scrawny."

"You could leave it on," April suggested.

"Everyone would say, 'Why is he swimming with his shirt on'."

"No one would say that. No one is here." In the distance, cars and trucks rumbled by on the Interstate. Then April added, "Well, *I'm* going to swim," and she jumped in.

In a few seconds he was in the pool, too, wearing his T-shirt, which ballooned with water and rose up around him. He smoothed the shirt down and swam. They played tag, darting back and forth, though after a short while they got out and sat by the edge with motel towels draped around their shoulders. April saw him notice her travel Scrabble, so she asked, "Do you play?"

But he shook his head. "No, sorry," he said.

"It's the greatest game," she said. "I basically live and breathe it."

"Show me how. I don't know anything."

For the next hour or so, April Blunt taught the boy how to play Scrabble. "Okay, here are the basics. There are one hundred tiles," she explained. "You pick seven and line them up on a rack. But I have a feeling that maybe you already know that."

"No," he said. "I actually don't."

She held out the bag, and he pulled out seven tiles and placed them on the rack she'd handed him.

"Now," April said, "you and your opponent take turns forming words on the board, just like in a crossword puzzle. Each letter of the alphabet has a point value, and a few letters are called 'power tiles,' because they're worth much more than the others." She explained the following:

The J was worth 8.

The Q was worth 10.

The X was worth 8.

And the Z was worth 10.

There were also two blanks in the game, she told him, and these were very important. "Blanks are a big deal," April said. "They help you make a lot of different words. You move the tiles to form words—unscrambled words are called anagrams. I sometimes see anagrams in my head at night," she added. "The letters jump around."

"What do you mean?"

"Well, I know this sounds majorly strange," April said. "But take the word INSTEAD. See, you can move the letters around so they spell SAINTED, or STAINED, or even DETAINS."

"Got it," he said.

"Plus," said April, "those same letters make a couple of other words that you've never heard of, like NIDATES and DESTAIN."

"Those are real?"

"I swear."

"This is pretty impressive," said the boy in the blue T-shirt.

"IMPRESSIVE," April said, "is an anagram of PERMISSIVE. And you know MARASCHINO?"

"Those cherries in drinks that no one really likes?"

April nodded. "MARASCHINO is an anagram of HARMONICAS."

The boy's mouth moved a little, as if he was arranging the letters silently. "You're right," he said.

She told him how if you used all the letters on your rack, it was called a bingo. And if you used all the letters of your rack *twice* in a row, it was called a bingo-bango. And if you used them *three times* in a row—

"Does that ever happen?" the boy interrupted. "Wouldn't it be, like, winning the *lottery* three times in a row?"

"It's never happened to me personally," April said, "but it definitely happens."

"Let me guess what it's called," said the boy. "Bingo-bango-*bungo*?"

"Close. Bingo-bango-bongo. And if you find a bingo but have nowhere to put it, it's called a homeless bingo."

"Poor homeless bingo," he said. "Just sort of wandering around with nowhere to live." The boy seemed to like hearing all these Scrabble facts, and as they began to play he picked up the rhythm of the game. She beat him in the end, but not by an insane amount.

Eventually the Blunt family came back to the motel. The blue van, with its bumper stickers that read: I'M A SPORTS LUNATIC, and HONK IF YOU LIKE HOCKEY, pulled into the lot, and the doors slid open and her family popped out, chugalugging water from plastic bottles. Her brother, Gregory, sucked the water out so fast that the plastic bottle became indented, making a loud popping sound. Her father saw April sitting by the pool, and he waved and came over.

"Hey, April," he said. "We're all going to take showers in the room, then grab a bite. Come with us."

She wished she could stay there with the boy. They were in the middle of a second game of Scrabble now, and he had been telling her about himself. He'd told her about going to a weeklong camp called Aller-ja-wee-a. "It was the corniest place," he said. "It was for kids who have food allergies—get it, *Aller-ja-wee-a?*—and I hated it. Any time we tried to do something on our own, a counselor was on our case."

"Sounds lame," April agreed.

"We had to play a game called Where Are the Nuts?" he said. "The counselors took us out into a field and hid little plastic objects in the grass that were supposed to represent nuts. We had to find them and throw them away like they were hand grenades about to go off."

April had told him how different she was from her jockish family. Now he could see that for himself. Her siblings and parents were all around the pool area, telling

April to hurry up and pack up her board and racks and score sheets.

"Can I have five more minutes to finish this game?" she asked her father. "Please, Dad?"

"Sure, why not," said her father. "I want to get a couple of snapshots of your brother anyway. You stay here, and I'll take some pictures." He took out his camera.

April's brother, Gregory, stood in front of her and the boy, saying, "Watch this!"

Still in his baseball uniform, Gregory turned a somersault off the side of the pool. The shutter snapped.

April said to the boy, "I've got an anagram for you. ROAST MULES."

"That's two words."

"I know. But if you unscramble the letters," April said, "it'll make one long word."

"Are you sure I know it?" he asked. "Maybe it's a word I've never seen before."

"You definitely know it," she said.

He thought and thought, but couldn't come up with the answer. Soon April's father told her it was really time to go. April said good-bye to the boy, and he said, "See you." Then she returned to the motel room, where her siblings wrestled on the beds and on the foldout sofa, and someone farted, making a *putt-putt* sound like a faraway car backfiring. Someone else laughed as if that fart were hilarious. Then someone turned on the TV, which was showing a game of *futbol* from Chile. Everyone in the family was happy to watch, except April.

When she peered through the heavy aqua drapes of the motel window a little while later, the boy was gone.

The next morning she'd looked for him in the breakfast room, where sleepy families sat drinking coffee and tea and hot chocolate, and eating cold rolls with butter and jam from tiny plastic packets. He wasn't there. Later, in the motel office at checkout, he still wasn't there. His family must have already left, April thought, disappointed. They must have already joined the line of cars heading out onto the Interstate.

Most kids who met when they were on a trip with their parents never saw each other again. The puppeteers took away the puppets. But even if they *did* see each other, they might not know it. You could meet someone when you were a kid, and then meet him again when you were both grown up, but you probably wouldn't even know it was the same person. April Blunt had met the boy in the blue T-shirt only once, and she knew nothing about him, but he still mattered to her after three years.

In April's bedroom now, sitting with Lucy, April said, "I never got to tell him the anagram of ROAST MULES."

"I'm sure it's kept him up all these nights," said Lucy.

"He probably *did* wonder about it at first," April said. But she worried, weirdly, that he had forgotten about ROAST MULES, and about meeting her.

"Tell me, Flink, what were the words on his T-shirt?" Lucy asked.

"I have no idea, Curnish."

"Think, Flink," Lucy said. "Maybe the words could give us a clue to his location. Maybe they could help you find him. Not that I totally understand why you even want to."

"I don't totally understand either," said April. "But even if I knew his location, it's not like I would recognize him. I barely remember what he looked like. And people's faces change a lot. Well, anyway, enough about this. We should get back to Scrabble. We want to make it to the finals so my family can finally *get* it. We want them to see us on *Thwap!* TV and be blown away."

"And we also want to win the ten thousand dollars," Lucy reminded her.

"Yes, that would be a plus."

"Let's go over the list of vowel dumps," Lucy said.

Vowel dumps were Scrabble words that used a lot of vowels. Even if you had what looked like a terrible rack, filled with A's, E's, I's, O's, and, worst of all, U's, there were many words that allowed you to get rid of extra vowels that had turned your rack into "Old MacDonald's Farm," as people said, which was a joke about it looking like EIEIO.

The vowel dump words were both ordinary and strange, and the four-letter ones included:

AEON

AGUE

AIDE

ALEE

ALOE

AQUA

AREA

ARIA

ASEA

AURA

AUTO

BEAU

CIAO

EASE

EAVE

EURO

IDEA

IOTA

LIEU

LUAU (This was April's favorite, because it got rid of *two* U's.)

MOUE

OBOE

OLEO
OOZE
OUZO
UREA

And the five-letter ones, which got rid of even more vowels, included:

ADIEU
AERIE
AUDIO
COOEE
EERIE
LOOIE
LOUIE
MIAOU
QUEUE

April and Lucy sat studying the word lists. "About the boy from the pool again," April suddenly said. "I'd like to try to find him one last time."

"Well, just see if you can remember the words on his shirt," said Lucy.

"I've done that," April said.

"All right then," said Lucy. "We'll try something else."

"What?"

"*You* know."

April did know. Lucy Woolery was an amateur hypnotist. She used an electric toothbrush with a spinning head, and she had successfully hypnotized her own father this way, getting him to walk around the house crumbling a piece of bread and dumbly repeating the words, "Bread is yummy. Bread is yummy."

When he came back to reality he was stunned to look down and see bread crumbs at his feet. Lucy had put a few other people into trances, too, including her cousin Wayne, and Ms. Gibney, the art teacher at school.

But not April. Even now, on the bed in April's room, with Lucy holding the spinning toothbrush in front of her face (she had it with her because she'd slept over the night before), saying, "Watch the toothbrush, April," it was clear that it wasn't going to work.

April just lay staring at it. "No offense, Luce," she said, "but is this going to go on much longer?"

Lucy finally clicked off the power switch. "Forget it, April," she said. "You're totally unhypnotizable. You're going to have to come up with another way to find him, wherever he is."

Chapter Five

THE CURSE OF THE ZYGOTES

The following week, far from April Blunt and far from Duncan Dorfman, on a cold, windy New York City street at eight A.M., Nate Saviano rode his skateboard toward the gates of school, his long dark hair sticking out beneath his helmet. All around him kids carried backpacks, or clutched science projects. A city bus rumbled past, and in it Nate could practically see down the throats of yawning kids. He could nearly see their uvulas, those things that looked like little punching bags in the back of everyone's throat.

UVULAS was a good Scrabble word to know, Nate thought.

It seemed that everyone in New York between the ages of five and eighteen was heading to school. But not Nate. The backpack strapped to his own back, covered with buttons and pins about skateboarding, was just for show; there was absolutely nothing inside it. He wanted people to think: *Oh look, there goes an ordinary kid heading to school.* But this wasn't true.

The wind picked up as Nate coasted toward P.S. 585 in lower Manhattan. Across the street from the school was a small and not particularly nice skate park where kids often went before and after the school day. A crowd had collected, and Nate joined them, just the way he used to when he was one of them.

He'd never expected that would ever change, and he'd been shocked when, before school started in September, his father had announced that Nate wouldn't be returning to P.S. 585. Instead, he was going to be homeschooled. "You'll learn a lot more at home," his father said.

"What?" said Nate. He couldn't believe it. "Who's supposed to be my teacher?" he asked.

"Me."

"You're not a teacher!" Nate shouted. And after that day, he began shouting at his father more and more. Larry Saviano was a science-fiction writer who had published a series of novels about the adventures of two astronauts traveling to the planet Zax, and who are whisked back in time. (ZAX was a Scrabble word; that was how Larry had come up with the name.)

Very few people had read the *Zax* novels. Even though Larry's books didn't make any money, the Savianos were far from poor. There was "money in the family," as his father sometimes said.

"I'm not a teacher, that's true, but I know a lot," said Larry.

"What does Mom say about this?" Nate asked.

"Oh, you know . . . She didn't love the idea at first, but I made her see that it could be a very positive experience for you."

Nate's mother lived uptown and had remarried a few years after the divorce. Her husband was a pediatrician, annoyingly known as "Dr. Steve." They had a baby named Eloise, and though the baby required a lot of attention, Nate's mother tried very hard to devote whole days to Nate. Once in a while she took him to the movies, or to Chinatown for soup dumplings, which actually had soup inside them. But often she was extremely busy.

"I wish I could be two places at once," she said as she fed the baby or made lunch or hurried off to her job as a pastry chef at a French restaurant.

So when Nate's father first offered to have Nate live

at his apartment during the school week, and stay at his mother's on weekends, the arrangement seemed like a good idea. The brainstorm about homeschooling had come later and had changed everything even more.

All around Nate now, kids tossed their backpacks into a pile and skated in the skate park during the narrow slice of time before school began. Nate added his own backpack to the pile and then turned and found himself face to face with TJ Wiles, who used to be his pretty good friend. "Yo, Nate!" said TJ, and the two of them slapped hands. "You're back?"

As he asked this, Maxie Roth zoomed over on her board. She had magenta hair and five tiny studs in one earlobe. She was as skinny as a boy, and she dressed like a boy, too, a skater boy, but her face was sharp and delicate. Her skateboard was pink with black stripes. She and Nate had started hanging out a little bit last year. They'd sat together in math class—both of them could do math in their heads superfast, and they both considered themselves skate freaks. Then the school year ended and Maxie had gone away to skate camp, and he hadn't seen her since then. She looked the same, but a little older, and maybe a little more . . . magenta.

"Is it true?" she asked Nate. "You're, like, back?"

"Nah," said Nate. "Just taking the skateboard out for a ride."

"Oh. Too bad," said Maxie. "It would've been fun to hang in math again," she said. "It would've been, like, fun to the tenth power," she added.

"The eleventh power," he said.

The other kids were starting to collect their things and head for school. "Hey, Roth; hey, Wiles—come on!" someone called, and TJ hurried off. Maxie gave Nate a crooked smile, pushing a bright piece of hair behind her ear, and then she said, "See you around, Nate," and was gone, too.

The cold and crummy little skate park was empty, and Nate felt as if he were the last kid on earth. His backpack was the only one that remained on the ground. Nate picked it up, looped it on, and headed home by himself. He didn't know why he felt as bad as he did. By the time he arrived at the front door of his apartment building, the streets of the city were quiet, all the kids off in school. All except one.

"Nathaniel Armstrong Saviano, is that you?" called his father as Nate let himself into the apartment.

It was, everyone said, an amazing place: enormous, with high ceilings and sunlight everywhere. After his father had come up with the idea of homeschooling Nate, he had added some features to the apartment that made it like a teenaged boy's dream house. The goal was to turn it into a place where Nate would want to spend all day. For starters, Larry had built an indoor skate park. There was room here to do ollies, heelflips, and half-cabs. It was so much nicer than the skate park across the street from the school, yet without other kids around, it seemed pointless.

Nate's father had also installed a sound studio with a little glassed-in room, some serious recording equipment, and a bunch of electric guitars that had once been owned by elderly rock stars Nate had never heard of. Larry had gone to such great lengths to make everything special that it was hard for Nate to let him know that he would have traded it all in if only he was allowed to go back to P.S. 585.

"Yeah, it's me, Dad," said Nate now, and he dropped into the ramp, then roared along the floor.

"Whoa, nice," said his father, who watched from the open kitchen, where he stood in his rumpled pajamas, making coffee. "I thought you were still asleep, kid."

"I got up early. Just wanted to get some air." Nate swung himself out of the skate park section of the apartment and flopped onto one of the low white couches that floated like islands in the middle of the room.

"Shoes off, please! Why do you have your backpack?" his father asked.

"I don't know," Nate said, working his sneakers off his feet and tossing them aside. He was too embarrassed to say that he had wanted to seem like a normal kid on his way to school.

"So let's pick up the lesson where we left off," said Larry. "What were we doing yesterday?"

"You mean, last night at midnight?" Nate asked, for his father had encouraged him to stay up late playing an online Scrabble game with a player from New Zealand called kiwiguy22. All evening Nate had been playing games online with anonymous people around the world.

Both of them knew the reason that Larry Saviano wanted his son to succeed. For twenty-six years, Larry had carried around the pain of having lost the Youth Scrabble Tournament when he was twelve. Larry and his partner, Wendell Bruno, had gone to Yakamee, Florida, together, and had made it all the way to the final round, which, to everyone's shock, they then lost. Their opponents had been a team of girls who had made the bingo ZYGOTES for their final move, leaving the two boys stunned and defeated.

The next time they sat down to play Scrabble, at Wendell's kitchen table back in Arizona, the game had literally made Larry sick. He had run to Wendell's bathroom and thrown up into the toilet and all over the little round blue bath mat on the floor. Larry vowed never to play again, and over all these years, he never did. Just the idea of sitting in front of a board made him want to throw up. His moment had come and gone.

But now his son's moment had arrived.

Of course it was immature that all these years later Nate's father had never gotten over it. But all Nate wanted now was to get him off his back, and the only way to do that was to go to the YST on December twelfth in Yakamee and avenge his father's loss. If he won the whole tournament, then Nate could be done with Scrabble forever. He would never have to look at another stupid tile. He would never have to think about bingos, or bingo-bangos, or bingo-bango-bongos.

One thing he needed was a partner. Nate didn't care who it was, since he'd only be going to the tournament to please his father. As far as he was concerned, he could have taken his *skateboard* with him, propped it on a chair, drawn a face on it, and called it his partner. But he would have to come up with a real person pretty soon, and it didn't even need to be someone who really played Scrabble.

Nate was planning on doing all the heavy lifting. His partner just had to sit there next to him. And then at the end, the two of them could split the ten-thousand-dollar first prize. Second prize was five thousand, and third prize was twenty-five hundred. Nate didn't need the money, and if his team won—which he knew they had to, and first place, not second or third—he planned to hand his winnings to one of the lowest-ranked teams. Then Nate Saviano would turn and head out the doors of the hotel ballroom where the tournament was held. His father would finally get over the past, and would allow Nate to return to P.S. 585.

But for now, Nate had to practice. "Yesterday," he wearily told his father, "we were doing singular Q words that don't take a U."

"Ah, yes," said Larry. He went to the refrigerator and poked his head inside. "How about some eggs?" he asked. "Brain food."

"So you've told me, Dad."

"You come up with a partner yet?" Larry asked.

"No."

"Well, please do. We have to send in the name. And now, while I cook, you recite."

"Do I have to?" Nate asked, but he knew the answer. "Okay," he began. "Now, this list is totally incomplete, but it's where I am so far. 'Singular Q words that don't take a U . . .'" he said, and he began to rattle off some words from memory:

"QABALA

QADI

QAID

QANAT

QAT

QI

QINDAR

QINTAR—"

"*QINTAR!*" his father cut in. "The things you know. It's just incredible."

"'Incredible' isn't the word I'd choose," Nate muttered. He was thinking more of "unbearable." Other kids his age often told Nate he was very lucky, and in some ways this was true. There were very few rules in the home school his father ran. If his mother ever found out how much freedom he had, she would make him live with her and Dr. Steve and Eloise full-time, instead of just on weekends.

Nate's father claimed that Nate was getting a great education. But the only learning that Larry Saviano really cared about was Scrabble. Sometimes in the evening, when Nate and his father were sitting around before bed, Nate could hear his father sadly say to himself, "ZYGOTES. Plural of ZYGOTE: a cell produced by two gametes. If only that girl had picked *one* different tile from the Scrabble bag! If only she had reached in and picked . . . *MYGOTES*."

"MYGOTES isn't a word, Dad," Nate would remind him.

"That's my point. If only she had picked MYGOTES, then Wendell and I would have won. My whole life would have been different."

Instead of being a writer whose *Zax* series had sold very few copies, Nate's father imagined that he would have been a famous author of bestsellers. "How would this have happened, Dad?" Nate wanted to ask, but he never did.

At first, homeschooling had been fun and interesting. One day a woman from the Board of Education came to the apartment to check out the situation. She had been impressed by the elaborate space that Nate's father had created, and she'd loved the science lab. "My! A skate park, too, Mr. Saviano," she'd said, shaking her head. "This will give Nate a chance to blow off steam during recess."

Recess? There *was* no recess! But she and Nate's father kept talking to each other as though this was actually a real school. Larry showed her the new talking globe he'd bought for Nate. You touched any country and a voice said something like, *"I—AM—YEMEN. MY—CAPITAL—IS—SANAA."*

On the kitchen table was an abacus. "I thought I would inject a little 'Asian flair' into math," his father told the woman. She nodded and said that the whole place seemed like "a magical exploratorium of learning." Whatever that meant.

But after the first couple of days the globe was never used, and the high-tech microscope grew filmy with dust. Even the sound studio remained an empty glass room, and the guitars of those former guitar heroes stayed silent. True, the skate park was still used frequently, but that didn't count.

Nate thought about how he and Maxie Roth used to work on problem sets together in class. He felt a twinge, missing that time. Other than math, very little actual *schooling* went on in his home once Scrabble took over. Nate didn't think his father had exactly planned it this way, but soon his days were Scrabble-filled.

Recently, Nate's father had taken him to a homeschooling convention to meet other kids and their families. One family lived in a van and traveled around the country attending indie-music festivals. "The *road* is our school," said the mother during a meet-and-greet session. She said her name was Sasha, and she introduced her "fellow life-traveler, Kick, and our kids Angelfire, Domino, and Burnt Sienna."

There were suburban families there, too, and ones who lived in neighborhoods where it was unsafe to walk to school. There were families who didn't want their kids learning about evolution. Other families simply thought their homes would be far more interesting environments for their kids than an actual school would be. Some families were very religious. Some were very *un*religious. In one family, the girls all wore bonnets.

"Hello, everyone. My name is Abigail," said a twelve-year-old girl in a bonnet. "My family and I bring thee good tidings and an offering of homemade jam." She held out a sticky jar with a slightly swollen lid, and passed it around with a bunch of spoons. Nate didn't really want to touch the jar when it was handed to him.

Mostly, though, the homeschooled families in the room seemed like anyone you would meet anywhere. When Nate thought about the old days—when his parents were still married, or even when he went to P.S. 585—his throat felt thick and a little choked.

During the week it was just Nate and his father. Larry Saviano would get up every so often during the day, pace around the apartment, and say in a vague voice, "How about history? Did you do any of it?"

"No."

"Why not?"

"You didn't give me an assignment, Dad."

"My bad. Read a few chapters in your history book," his father would say. "And once you're done with that—what was the subject, the Native Americans?—when you're done with the Native Americans, get back to studying."

"But that *is* studying."

"You know I mean studying Scrabble words."

Once, as a joke, Nate made a sign and taped it up facing outward on one of the windows in the apartment. It read, HELP!!! I AM A CHILD BEING FORCED TO PLAY SCRABBLE ALL DAY WHEN I SHOULD BE IN SCHOOL!!!!

A neighbor who'd been out walking his dog came upstairs and knocked on the door. "Everything okay in there?" he asked. He insisted on poking his head inside, as if he'd imagined he might see a kid handcuffed to a Scrabble board. "Wow, this is quite a place," the neighbor said. He turned to Nate. "You must be like the *opposite* of a prisoner in here!"

"Yes, my son's just a big, hilarious joker," said Larry. "He cracks everyone up, especially me! Thanks so much for your concern, but as you can see, everything's great."

When the neighbor and his dog left, Larry turned to Nate with a hurt expression. "You know that I give you plenty of freedom, right?"

But Nate didn't think that was true. He didn't care about Scrabble—actually, more and more, he *hated* it. It didn't make him sick the way it made his father sick, but the games he was going to play at the YST would be his last. All he wanted now was to win first prize and be done for good.

Maybe, then, his father would let go of the lifelong pain of having lost his own tournament—his glory stolen away all because of the word ZYGOTES. Maybe his father would finally agree that it was time to let Nate back out into the world.

On the weekend, Nate Saviano took the subway to his mother and stepfather's apartment uptown. There was no indoor skate park, no recording studio. It was just an ordinary household centered around the raising of a baby. Ugly plastic toys were scattered around, and kiddie music played.

When Nate walked in now, he could hear a song by some annoying children's singer called Kazoo Stu. The song went:

"And if you DON'T take the kangaroo outta my hair/I'm gonna have to dress him up in Daddy's un-der-weeeeaar . . ."

Which was followed by a lot of kazoo playing.

Nate hesitated in the doorway; he knew what awaited him this weekend. It wasn't just that his mother's apartment was so hectic, but also that, whenever he was here, he felt as if he was being watched.

"Just *look* at him," his mother said now to her husband. Dr. Steve was a nice guy, but he talked to everyone as if they were five years old. He was always on the phone with worried parents. No matter what time of day it was, Nate could hear him say, "Be sure she drinks plenty of fluids."

"Hey there, Nate," said Dr. Steve. "Come a little closer so I can get a better look at you. Your mom says you're run-down."

Nate dropped his weekend bag and skateboard and reluctantly walked over. Dr. Steve took a good look at him, putting both hands on either side of Nate's neck, checking for swollen glands.

"I'm *fine*, Steve," Nate said.

"I'm just going to palpate your glands."

PALPATE, Nate thought. That was a new word for him; he would have to remember to try and play it sometime.

"You getting enough sleep?" asked Dr. Steve. "That's very important for tweens."

Nate hated the word TWEENS, even though it was a good Scrabble word. "Yeah," Nate lied. He had actually only slept for five hours the night before. He would have liked to go lie down right that minute, but it wasn't possible.

61

He had to share a bedroom here with Eloise, and she was screaming in her crib.

"I don't believe you, Nate," said his mother. "I think your dad is making you stay up late at night. Nate, tell me the truth."

"Dad is being fine," Nate said.

But soon she was on the phone, saying, "No, you listen to *me*, Larry—he is *twelve*. He has to just be a kid. He can't make you feel better. Oh, he *can*? Well, he shouldn't *have* to make you feel better. You're a grown-up now. You know what?" she said. "Steve and Eloise and I are going to come along to that tournament on December twelfth, so we can stay on top of everything."

"What?" said Nate, but his mother waved him away from the phone.

He didn't want them coming to the YST! Dr. Steve would go up to random players and palpate the glands in their necks. Eloise would explode foul-smelling stuff into her diaper during a tense moment in a Scrabble game. His mother would get into an argument with his father in front of everyone. They didn't belong down there. But Nate's mother still felt uncomfortable leaving him with his Scrabble-obsessed father all the time, and she wanted to show that she was a very involved parent, too. Which she was.

When she got off the phone, she said, "Okay, so it's all settled."

"No," said Nate. "It's not. It's not settled!"

"Inside voice, Nate, inside voice," said Dr. Steve.

"It's just that I don't need you guys going down there with Dad and me. Really, I'll be fine."

"We want to come," said his mother. "Besides, it'll make for a nice family vacation. Isn't Yakamee, Florida, where that weird amusement park is?"

"That's right," said Dr. Steve. "Funswamp."

"Funswamp?" said Nate. "I've never heard of it."

"It's an amusement park built completely on swampland," said Dr. Steve. "They've got a gator coaster."

Nate shook his head, defeated. He knew he would have to let them come.

"Who's your partner going to be, Nate?" asked his mother.

"Maxie Roth," he answered without thinking; her name had just jumped out of him. Maxie Roth, the ultra-cool skater girl with the magenta hair and multipierced earlobe. The girl who liked to ride fast and do mental math. As far as he knew, she had no interest in Scrabble. But suddenly, he thought, if I have to go to the YST, then maybe she can go, too. He would text her later and ask her to be his partner.

All Nate wanted—and all that he thought about, many times each day—was that he had to get by until the YST, win first prize, then shout at his father, "Are you finally *happy*?" At which point he would add, "And can I please go back to school already?"

But now, an awful thought occurred to Nate. For some reason, it had almost never occurred to him before.

What if he didn't win?

Chapter Six

THE LESSONS BEGIN

"Did you know that SPORK is no good?" Carl Slater asked Duncan Dorfman on a cold afternoon in late October. School was out for the day, and the two boys sat at Slice's, the pizza place in downtown Drilling Falls.

"No. I did not know that," said Duncan.

"You might have assumed that SPORK is perfectly fine, right? After all, you've used a *spork* before—one of those plastic spoon-forks. But the Scrabble people say nope, sorry, it ain't good, at least not yet."

"Huh," said Duncan. "What do you know."

"And then there are plenty of words that you *wouldn't* think were good, but they are," said Carl. "Your job is to move letters around until you make real words out of them." Carl took a bite of pizza, which dripped about a quart of orange oil onto his plate. "Words are like clay, Dorfman," he went on. "They can be shaped and messed with not only by your hands, but also by your *head*. So if you want to win at Scrabble, you have to learn how to move words around and totally reshape them. Do you get what I'm saying?"

Duncan nodded. Once in a while the front door of the pizza place would swing open and the little bell would ring, and one of Carl Slater's friends would see Carl and start to say, "Hey, dude, what are you—" Then he would notice who Carl was sitting with, and understand that a lesson was taking place. "Catch you later," the friend would say, backing out. Most of Carl's friends were annoyed by Duncan, because he hogged all of Carl's attention these days.

Carl Slater was seen as the king of the Drilling Falls Scrabble Club. If someone had a question about whether a word was good or not, they went to Carl. Brian Kalb was particularly unfriendly toward Duncan now, since Duncan had replaced him as Carl's partner at the upcoming tournament in Florida. Because Brian had gone with Carl last year, he had assumed they would go together again this year. It wasn't fair that Brian had been elbowed aside by Duncan, a total beginner, but this was the way Carl wanted it.

Carl Slater had become Duncan's Scrabble tutor. "I can take a total word dummy like yourself—no offense, man—and turn you into a major player," he'd said.

Ever since the day in the cafeteria when Duncan had revealed his so-called power, Carl had taken it upon himself to show Duncan "the ropes," as he called it. "I could also say, 'show you the PROSE,'" he added.

"What?" said Duncan.

"PROSE is an anagram of ROPES. Oh, and SPORE is too. And POSER."

In the hall closet of Aunt Djuna's house, among the boxes that Duncan and his mother had brought with them on the bus from Michigan, was a Scrabble set. It was the old-fashioned kind, in a rectangular maroon box, and it had once belonged to his mother, though she never played it anymore. The day that Duncan started playing with Carl, he'd gone into the closet and taken out the box. Inside was the board, folded in half. Also in the box was an old piece of lined paper with oily spots on it, on which a game had been scored a long time ago.

Duncan had recognized his mother's handwriting. One of the players had been written down as "Caroline." That was his mother. The other one, Duncan saw from the faded ink, had been written down as "Ms."

"Who's 'Ms'?" Duncan had asked his mother.

"Ms? What do you mean?" she said.

He showed her the name written on the score sheet, and his mother stood looking at it. "Oh," she said quietly, taking the sheet from him. She paused. "'*Ms.*' That was my teacher, Ms. Thorp. We played sometimes."

"Ms. Thorp beat you," said Duncan, noticing that the final scores were 382 to 261.

"So she did. I remember that she was a good player," Caroline Dorfman said. She walked into the kitchen, crumpled up the score sheet, and threw it into the garbage under the sink.

So now, as October in Drilling Falls neared its end, Duncan was becoming a good player, too.

Carl didn't really care whether or not Duncan actually *liked* Scrabble. Carl simply wanted to bring him to the tournament. And it was only because of the sensitivity of Duncan's fingertips. Duncan was going to be Carl's partner so that during the games Duncan could pick both blanks, all four S's, and all the power tiles from the bag. Not to mention the four-point H's and W's, and the five-point K. Or even just so Duncan could pick combinations of letters that could make bingos and earn his team a ton of points.

"Also, Dorfman," Carl reminded Duncan as they sat in the pizza place with their slices in front of them, the oil making the paper plates look almost see-through, "don't forget that Scrabble is not just about picking good letters, or finding anagrams. You also have to know how to look at your rack."

"What do you mean?"

"For instance, when you have an E and a D, you should automatically put them at the end of your rack, hoping that you can make a word that ends in ED. The same is true of ING. And, of course, if you have an S, you should see if it can make a plural. And if you have EST, well, that could be an ending, too. But then again so could TCH, like in the word CATCH. Got it?"

"Sort of," said Duncan.

"This is true of the beginnings of words, too. You should try to cluster consonants together on your rack, if you have them. Like TH, or CH, or SH. And there are plenty of others. You still with me?" Duncan nodded. "Okay, good. But the most important thing—like basically knowing how to tie your own *shoes*—is knowing your twos."

"My what?" said Duncan, his mouth full of pizza.

"Your two-letter words. Every serious Scrabble player learns them, and I have decided that today you are ready. You have to memorize the list," Carl said. "I guarantee that if you learn these words, your game will improve a million percent." Carl reached into his pocket and pulled out a folded piece of paper. He smoothed it down on a clean part of the table. "Here you go," he said. "Read it. Learn it. Or, hey, just rub it with the fingertips of your left hand, in your case."

But Duncan didn't want to use his fingertips to study the list. He wanted to memorize it the way everyone else did. Since that day in the cafeteria, he had almost never used his fingertips again. He sensed that they were meant for big occasions only. Now that he knew his skill was something of value, he didn't take it lightly.

He glanced down the list of twos, which was partly made up of words that he had never seen or heard before. But all of these words were acceptable in a game of Scrabble:

AA
AB
AD
AE
AG
AH
AI
AL
AM
AN
AR
AS

AT

AW

AX

AY

BA

BE

BI

BO

BY

DE

DO

ED

EF

EH

EL

EM

EN

ER

ES

ET

EX

FA

FE

GO

HA

HE
HI
HM
HO
ID
IF
IN
IS
IT
JO
KA
KI
LA
LI
LO
MA
ME
MI
MM
MO
MU
MY
NA
NE
NO
NU

OD

OE

OF

OH

OI

OM

ON

OP

OR

OS

OW

OX

OY

PA

PE

PI

QI

RE

SH

SI

SO

TA

TI

TO

UH

UM

UN
UP
US
UT
WE
WO
XI
XU
YA
YE
YO
ZA

"Whoa!" Duncan said when he got all the way to ZA. "I have to *memorize* all of these? That's insane, Carl. I'm not good at that."

"Then what are you good at?" Carl asked.

Duncan was silent. He knew, actually, that he was not particularly good at anything. Nothing had come together inside him and grabbed him by the throat. He had no burning interest yet; he still had no incredible ability in any subject at school or in any sport. Suddenly he felt babyish and ashamed.

"I don't know yet," said Duncan.

"Well," said Carl, "just memorize these twos. Become good at it. I swear," he went on, "it's no harder than some of the things you have to memorize for school. Like last year in science we had to learn all these unfamous parts of the human body. Did you know that we've got things inside us called the islets of Langerhans?"

"No," said Duncan. You could never tell, with Carl Slater, whether he was being serious or trying to jerk you around.

Duncan folded the list back up and put it into his own pocket. Sitting here across the table from Carl, he thought about what a long way he had come since the earliest days of school, when he was simply Lunch Meat, lumped together with the Chinaman. His ordinariness and dullness now seemed increasingly far away. As far away as the islets of Langerhans.

LANGERHANS, Duncan thought as he sat in Slice's. He moved the letters around slowly in his mind, as Carl had told him to do. He saw that you could make HANGERS from LANGERHANS. Or, he saw, you could make LASAGNE. You'd still have leftover letters, of course, but hey, Duncan joked to himself, you *always* have leftovers when you make lasagne.

"The thing is, dude," said Carl, "it's one thing for you to be able to *feel* the tiles and know what they are. I mean, it's a great skill, because as I said, you can pull all the best tiles out of the bag. And your opponent will basically be left with a rack made up of EEEIIOA." He snickered softly.

"Or VWULNUG. But once you've *got* the tiles, you still need to keep up your side of the game. I can't do everything by myself," he added. "I'm good, but there are kids out there across the country who are a lot better. And we're all going to meet up in Yakamee. Last year Drilling Falls got humiliated—it was *pathetic*—but this year, with my secret weapon by my side, we will cream everyone."

"What's your secret weapon?" Duncan asked, and as soon as he spoke, he thought: DUH. (A word, he had recently found out, that was good in Scrabble.)

"*You* are, dude," said Carl Slater cheerfully. "You're my secret weapon. And I forgot to mention this, but when we win that money, I will be happy to split it with you seventy-thirty. That would net you *three thousand dollars*. Pretty nice pay for doing something you do anyway—feeling things on flat surfaces, right? I know your mom could really, really use that money," he added. Carl stood, shrugging into his denim jacket. "Speaking of moms," he said, "I see that mine has just pulled up outside. I've got to run."

Duncan looked through the pizza-place window and saw a gleaming black sports car with an ornament of a leaping gazelle on its hood. Inside was a woman who had an older, female version of Carl Slater's face, with slightly puffy-looking lips. She was smoking a cigarette, which clouded the inside of the car. She pressed a button to lower the window, and some of the smoke escaped. "CARL!" she called in a hoarse voice. "ORTHODONTIST'S! NOW!"

"See you," Carl said to Duncan. "Work on those twos. And think about the cash, my friend."

Duncan Dorfman understood that Carl Slater wasn't really his friend. Anyone could see that a seventy-thirty split was unfair. Anyone could hear the casual unpleasantness in Carl's line about how Duncan's mother could really, really use that money.

"Sounds good to me," Duncan said.

I am a doormat, he thought. I am Duncan Doormat. And I am also an old piece of lunch meat that's lying on the doormat, and someone is stepping on it and squashing it forever.

"So it's a deal," said Carl. "Seventy-thirty. Seventy me, thirty you. Obviously."

"It's a deal," Duncan heard himself reply. Though he hated himself for saying it, the words were already out of his mouth.

And words, he realized, mattered.

Chapter Seven

THE SEARCH FOR THE BOY FROM NOWHERE

On a Friday night in November, April Blunt and Lucy Woolery babysat together for an extremely hyper four-year-old named Jasper Kroger, who lived across the street from the Woolerys. After insisting that April and Lucy cook him some packaged clown-head-shaped macaroni and cheese, then create a scavenger hunt for him throughout the house, and finally call his father's cell phone to ask how old he would have to be to get a tattoo ("Thirty-five," Mr. Kroger calmly replied), little Jasper finally collapsed while listening to a CD of some annoying kiddie singer who played the kazoo, and April and Lucy had a chance to talk. The school week had been very busy, but now that the weekend had come, they wanted to discuss the upcoming Scrabble tournament, and also, once again, the boy from the motel pool.

"Any brainstorms about finding him?" Lucy asked.

"Nope," April said.

They were sitting in the Krogers' playroom, on child-sized chairs at a child-sized table, beneath a big painting of a dinosaur on a unicycle, eating Jasper's leftover clown-head macaroni and cheese, which was an orange color so bright and unnatural that it almost hurt to look at it. *Now with even more disgusting neon flavor!* April thought the package should have read. A few days earlier, they had gone online and tried to locate the summer camp for allergic kids that the boy at the pool had told her he'd gone to, but apparently it no longer existed.

"If we're seriously ever going to make any progress locating him," said Lucy, "then we're going to have to come up with a new plan." Of course, neither of them had a plan in mind, so they sat eating the rubbery macaroni for a minute or two, thinking hard.

When their plates were empty, April said, "I've got nothing. You?"

"Nothing," said Lucy.

They stopped thinking about the boy for now. Instead they took out the Scrabble set that Lucy had brought with her, set it up on the tiny table, then bent over it and began to play.

The next morning, when April Blunt awoke and went downstairs in her house, the place was in full swing. This was always the case; her family woke up earlier than she did. They woke up earlier than *anyone*, except maybe farmers. A ball was hitting a wall somewhere deep in the distance, with a rhythm that made the whole house shudder. Her brother, Gregory, came skating in on his Rollerblades, dressed in full hockey gear, knocking a little puck along the floorboards.

"You'll leave wheel marks, Gregory," April said. She was often in a cranky mood when she woke up and had to face the sports world of her family.

"Just because you don't know how to Rollerblade doesn't mean you have to take it out on me," Gregory said, and he pivoted and glided away, leaving a wheel mark in the place where the hallway opened into the living room.

"Maybe I don't want to Rollerblade!" she called out to him. "Maybe I have other things to do!" But Gregory was already in an entirely different part of the house, probably leaving wheel marks there, too.

Jenna, the older of April's two sisters, was sitting on the living room couch studying a notebook in which were written plays for her touch football game that weekend. April's other sister, Liz, was doing stretches on the floor, hoping that a charley horse in her left leg would heal before lacrosse tomorrow.

"Scrabble's a sport, too," April said to the room in general. It was something she had said many times before, but it never made a dent.

Jenna looked up from the sheet of diagrams so complicated they seemed like something a mad scientist would write on a blackboard. "What?" she asked through her haze of concentration.

"I said that Scrabble's a sport," said April.

"So you've told us," said Liz with a little half smile, before returning to her stretching.

April headed down the hall, passing her mother, who was on her hands and knees, her head in a closet, searching for something.

"Hi, Mom," April said.

"Oh hi, babe, you're up," said her mother, backing out of the closet. "Good. Breakfast's in a minute. Everyone's starving. Have you seen Gregory's mouth guard?"

"What? No," April answered.

"Well, if you do—"

"Okay, fine, got it," said April, and she went into the dining room and sat down at the big wooden table, not wanting to think about a little lost black piece of rubber with her brother's tooth marks and germs all over it. In the quiet room before her family arrived, she thought instead about Scrabble words. Yawning, April put her head down on the table and let her mind get loose and dreamy. Soon, different words appeared before her. A couple of random, strange Scrabble words drifted past. She saw:

GARDYLOO

and . . .

ILEX

and . . .

SILEX

April must have fallen back asleep, she realized, because the next thing she knew, everyone was all around her, and her dad was bringing a mess of pancakes to the table, and her brother was saying, "I want a ton of syrup, Dad. Like, an entire reservoir." All the Blunts did seem to be starving, and why not? Most of them had been up since dawn, running laps or lifting weights or doing sit-ups. As usual in this family, everyone talked at once.

When there was a brief quiet moment, April said, "Lucy and I practiced for the tournament last night."

"Which tournament?" asked Liz.

"Scrabble," said April. There was no reply.

"Well, that's nice," her father finally said. "You girls work hard at that word game."

April's face got warm again, but it was from frustration instead of embarrassment. She knocked back a glass of OJ to cool herself down. Too bad OJ wasn't good in Scrabble. Why couldn't her family understand the thrill of Scrabble, the excitement when you won a game, or even when you made an amazingly interesting word?

She flashed back once again to the boy in the blue T-shirt at the motel pool. Somehow, she knew that he would have understood how she felt. Maybe, April thought, he had even gone on to become really good at Scrabble. And maybe every time he played it now, he remembered the redheaded girl who had taught him.

"Here's a good thing to know in Scrabble," April told her family. She looked around the table and saw that all of them except her mother had resumed eating, their heads bent down. She could see the parts in her sisters' and her brother's hair, and half of the bald circle on the very top of her father's head.

"Go on, sweetie," said her mother. "We're listening. What did you want to say?"

"Nothing," said April.

"Come on," said her father, looking up. Most likely, April thought, her mother had given him a kick under the table. "Tell us."

"It's a trick for knowing what letters can go after the letters K-A," she said. "Just remember BETSY'S FEET." Everyone looked at her blankly. "The letters in the words

BETSY'S FEET are the only ones that can go after the letters K-A in a game of Scrabble," April said. "That means you could make every word that I'm about to say."

She took a breath, then rattled off:

"KAB

KAE

KAF

KAS

KAT

KAY."

Her family continued to look as blank as a set of blank tiles. "Those are actual words?" her mother asked, and April nodded. "Have you ever heard of KAB or KAF?" she asked her husband.

"Nope," he said. "Never have."

"Neither have I."

"Neither have we," said Liz and Jenna, and a second later Gregory chimed in, too. Then, satisfied that they had given April enough time to talk about what interested her, they all began a discussion about the pros and cons of different brands of cleats.

After breakfast, when her father and her siblings were out in the yard, April sat alone in the den. It was a comfortable, woodsy room with a dark red couch that you could sink into, which was what she did now. She thought again about the boy in the T-shirt from the motel pool. She didn't even know what she would say to him if she found him. What could she say? *So, um, like, what's been new with you over the past three years?* Probably their conversation would be awkward, and he would think she was peculiar for wanting to track him down.

But she knew she didn't have to worry about this, because she was never going to find him.

April lay on the couch with her hands linked under her head and looked around the room. There were books stuffed into the shelves, and sports trophies on every surface. On the shelf beneath the coffee table was a stack of photo albums that her family had looked through many times over the years. Each one had gold printing on its spine. One read, THE BLUNT KIDS—ICE HOCKEY. Another read, THE BLUNT KIDS—LACROSSE. April had patiently sat and looked at these albums while her siblings gave her a blow-by-blow account of everything that was happening in each picture. She'd seen them all before, but now something—a little jab of a thought—made her want to see them again. Maybe she could find something in one of them.

Within seconds April had pulled out an album. The words on the spine read, THE BLUNT KIDS—BASEBALL AND SOFTBALL. April sat down with it in the big leather armchair, swiftly turning the stiff, plastic-sealed pages, looking at photos of her brother and sisters in uniform. In one shot,

Liz was catching a fly ball; in another, Gregory was sliding into home. April realized that she knew what she was looking for, but she didn't actually think she would find it.

Then, on the second to last page, she did.

In front of her was a snapshot of Gregory in a baseball uniform doing a somersault into a pool. Her mother had labeled the photo, GREGORY SHOWING OFF. But Gregory wasn't the person April was looking at.

In the background of the photo she could see a blurry image of herself, a few years younger, on a lounge chair in a bathing suit with a portable Scrabble set. Sitting across from her, also blurry, was the boy from the motel pool.

April opened her mouth, but no sound came out. This photograph had been here *for three years*, and yet until this second April hadn't known it existed. Probably, she thought, her own face appeared in the background of other families' vacation photos, a brief and random visitor in their lives.

She continued to stare at the boy. Though she could hardly make out his face, the white writing on his blue T-shirt was clear enough. It read: SETTLE MARS.

What a strange phrase to put on a T-shirt. April was surprised she hadn't remembered it before now. Within seconds, she was back upstairs in her room, and she and Lucy were on the phone, whispering frantically. Lucy, who always had her laptop open in front of her, was a very fast Internet searcher.

"'SETTLE MARS,'" Lucy murmured as she typed. "'SETTLE MARS.' Do you think it could be a command? Or even the name of a band? I've heard of a grunge band called Eat My Tinfoil." Lucy's computer keys clicked away. "Wait. *Got it*," she said, and then she read aloud: "'Settle Mars' is an organization that believes we should settle the planet Mars, which holds so much promise for mankind, since the earth has become so damaged by global warming."

"Well, that's depressing," said April.

"'Meetings are held in the basement of the Bakersfield, California, Public Library,'" Lucy went on. "A bunch of Mars-loving people in a library basement? That's depressing, too. I wonder if they dress up in green, and speak in a language with chirps and beeps."

"Why are you reading me this?" asked April. "I don't get it."

"Don't you *see*?" said Lucy. "The boy at the pool could be a member of this group. And maybe now," she added, "you'll finally be able to find him. And go see him again, and say to him . . . whatever you want to say to him."

The next day after school, sitting in Lucy's kitchen, April dialed the California phone number of Settle Mars. A woman answered, her voice pleasant if a little strange.

"Hello," said April. "I have just been reading about your organization, and I was thinking of joining."

"Do you live in the Bakersfield area?" asked the woman.

"Uh, nearby," April lied. "Are there any members who might be about my age? I'm in the . . . almost-teenaged category," she said.

"I should say not," said the woman. "We are not some kind of after-school kids' club. We are a respected group that entertains the highest scientific inquiries about the red planet. The earth is on its way out. Mars is the new earth."

And with that, the woman rudely hung up.

At some point in the near future, April Blunt thought, humans might certainly colonize Mars. But for now, it seemed impossible to do something as simple as find a boy from a motel pool, a boy who lived somewhere—but who knew where?—on earth.

April turned to Lucy and said in a defeated voice, "He's not in the group."

For a second, Lucy didn't answer. But then she said, "What if he's in another group?"

"What?"

"What if he's a member of his school's Scrabble team? After all—and basically it's our only hope—you did make him love Scrabble. It might have *stuck*."

"Well, that's a nice idea, and I've thought of it before, but I still wouldn't be able to find him."

"That isn't necessarily true."

"What are you saying?" April asked.

"Maybe," said Lucy, "you will find him on December twelfth."

Chapter Eight

SMOOTH MOVES

All fall, ever since that astonishing morning in the school cafeteria, Duncan Dorfman had relied on his fingertips only twice, both times during Scrabble games against Carl Slater. Carl wanted Duncan to use them every time they played, "to get you in the habit," he said, but Duncan refused. He was saving his ability, his "power," for December twelfth. "And even at the YST," Duncan had warned Carl repeatedly, "I'm only planning on using my fingertips when absolutely necessary."

"Yeah, sure, whatever," said Carl.

"I mean it," said Duncan. "Okay, Carl?"

"Okay. Relax."

One afternoon in late November, thirteen days before the tournament, Carl invited Duncan to play a few games at his house after school. Though they had been practicing all the time, they had always gone to Slice's, setting up the travel set on a table in the back. But today Slice's was closed for renovations, so Carl suggested they walk to his house instead.

Carl Slater lived in a section of Drilling Falls called The Inlet, which was surrounded by high metal gates covered with ivy and had its own security booth. Carl waved to the security guard and he and Duncan walked through. Each house in The Inlet looked as if it should have been on the cover of a magazine called *Rich People's Life*.

"See that one?" Carl said, pointing in the direction of an enormous house set way back from the road. "Well, you can hardly see it, but you know who lives there? Thriftee Mike. The real guy."

"Really?" said Duncan. "That's my mom's boss. Or anyway, the boss of her boss. Not that she's ever met him. I heard he only comes into the store at night, when everyone's gone."

"Yeah, I heard that, too. I haven't met him either," said Carl. "He's not very friendly, apparently. He lives there by himself, and he spends a lot of money on security for his house and stuff. I guess he's not really all that thrifty."

The Slater house, down the street from Thriftee Mike's, was massive and white, with tall columns out front. In the driveway sat Carl's mother's black sports car, and on the hood was the leaping gazelle ornament that seemed to coax the car forward like a horse pulling a chariot.

CHARIOT, Duncan thought, was an anagram of HARICOT, which was a green bean. He had been picking up new words fast. A lot of them were simply *words* to him, but he had already learned the meanings of some of the weirder ones, and he'd started trying to use them in conversation.

"Oh," said Carl. "I guess my mom's home."

Inside, the black-and-white hallway of the Slater house seemed to go on for a while, and the only objects in it were a few statues of the heads of Slater ancestors. On the wall was an enormous painting of Carl and his parents standing on the lawn, all dressed up and looking off into the distance unhappily. Carl's father was a businessman who traveled a lot, Carl said.

"Carl! Carl! Is that you?" called Mrs. Slater from down the hall. There came the sound of clacking heels as she made her way toward the boys, a cigarette waving in her hand. "Oh," she said, "you've brought home a friend." When Duncan was introduced, she said, "Yes, Carl's Scrabble partner."

"That's me," said Duncan. He liked the way "Scrabble partner" sounded. Of course, Carl probably made fun of

Duncan to Brian Kalb (who still hated Duncan for replacing him at the upcoming tournament) and Mitchell Farley and Tiffany Griggs and the others when Duncan wasn't around, calling him Lunch Meat—perhaps even singing little mean songs about him that included the words "Lunch Meat." But right now, Duncan almost imagined that he was Carl's real friend.

"You boys want a snack?" asked Mrs. Slater. "We've got Hoo-Has in the pantry."

Hoo-Has! Duncan's mother never bought those kind of sugary treats ("High fructose corn syrup? Seventeen grams of fat? Are you out of your *mind*?" she'd say in the supermarket when Duncan handed her a box to put in the cart.), but Duncan wished she would, at least once in a while. And *pantry*? Who had a pantry?

Carl Slater's mother said, "Remind your mom that she needs to send me that check."

"What check?" asked Duncan.

"*The* check," said Carl's mother impatiently. "For the tournament."

"Oh, sorry, dude," said Carl. "I didn't tell you about this? I guess it slipped my mind."

"Carl, I distinctly remember telling you that you had to ask your partner to give you a check," said Mrs. Slater. "It's so I can be paid back for the registration fee for the YST, which I've already sent in, as well as for the special rate on the hotel rooms at the Grand Imperial. And, of course, the airfare."

Registration fee?

Hotel rooms?

Airfare?

Why hadn't Duncan thought about any of this before? He had been so excited by the whole thing that until this second he hadn't really wondered how he and Carl were going to get down to Florida, or even where they would stay. Or how any of it would be paid for. He had daydreamed all the time about winning first place and bringing home the prize money. He'd imagined walking through the halls of school as if he were a popular football player in a uniform that said The Drilling Falls Dobermans; or even the middle school president—a slick kid who everyone high-fived. In this fantasy, Duncan was someone who would never be called Lunch Meat again. "Lunch Meat?" someone would say. "We were wrong to throw a piece of baloney at you, man. You didn't deserve that at all. A million apologies. You're *awesome*."

All Duncan had told his mother was that he had joined the Scrabble Club, and that he and his partner, Carl, were planning to go to a tournament in Florida. He had let her think what she wanted; and what she thought was that the tournament and all extra costs would be paid for by the school. She knew nothing about the fingertips part of the story. Just as she and Aunt Djuna had their whispered secrets at night, Duncan had *his* secrets, and his mother knew nothing about them.

He had tried to put it all out of his mind. Instead, he'd been focusing on learning to play well.

"The total amount," said Mrs. Slater coolly now, "is eight hundred and eighty-five dollars."

Duncan certainly couldn't tell his mother *that*, even though he and Carl stood a very good chance of winning a lot more than eight hundred and eighty-five dollars by the time the weekend was over.

But Duncan had to get to that tournament. If he didn't go, he would return to being an invisible nothing at school. He would be Lunch Meat forever. He would be no one, and he would have nothing. He wouldn't get his portion of the prize money, and he and his mother would never get to move into their own home. He would be a person of no significance.

Scrabble would save him; it had to. Sometimes at his great-aunt's house he went into the hall closet and took out his mother's old maroon Scrabble set, then he sat at the kitchen table by himself and moved the letters around on the board, thinking more deeply than he ever had in his life.

"Okay," Duncan said to Mrs. Slater in a small voice. "I'll let my mom know."

Carl shot his mother a look, then mouthed something to her behind his hand. She mouthed something back. They stood in front of Duncan, talking behind their hands. Then Carl said, "Listen, Duncan. Just in case you don't have the eight hundred and eighty-five right now, here's a way to make it work. My mom and I have discussed this, and she wants to say something."

"If paying me back is a problem, Duncan," Mrs. Slater said, "I would like to offer you a job."

"A job?"

At age twelve, Duncan Dorfman had never held a job, unless you counted raking leaves in Aunt Djuna's tiny front yard, which Duncan had done for free every weekend that fall.

"Yes," said Carl's mother. "I work in advertising. One of my clients is a company that needs a great campaign. You know what a campaign is?"

"I'm not sure," he said.

"It's a way of getting people to know a product. We want to put up ads on billboards and at bus stops. We thought we'd start advertising locally, and see how it goes. I was thinking that the ads could feature you and Carl playing a game together. Of course, we wouldn't show an actual *Scrabble* board, because that's not allowed. And after all, this isn't an ad for Scrabble. But we could make the board look kind of blurry, and show you and Carl concentrating hard. You would just be two wholesome boys playing a friendly game of . . . whatever."

Duncan thought about it, then said, "That sounds okay, Mrs. Slater."

"Isn't that great," she said, stubbing out her cigarette in an ashtray that had been hidden behind one of the statues. "If you do the photo shoot, consider the whole weekend in Florida taken care of. You and your mom won't have to pay a penny."

Duncan was relieved about the money, and he and Carl went upstairs and began to play. They sat on the floor of Carl's room, which was decorated to look like the inside of a ship, with a porthole for a window, and brass rails. Duncan and Carl sprawled out on the ocean-blue rug, eating Hoo-Has. It was obvious to both of them that Duncan was getting rapidly better at Scrabble, even without using his fingertips to pull the best tiles from the bag.

"But, dude, once you actually do use your crazy talent at the tournament," said Carl, "then we will *rule*."

Ever since they'd become partners, Carl had tried to convince Duncan that using his fingertips during the tournament wouldn't be cheating. "Chill out," he said whenever Duncan worried about it, or reminded Carl that he was uncomfortable about the whole thing, or that he was only planning on using his power as infrequently as possible. "I hear you," said Carl. "I know you're nervous. But just remember that you won't be using a cheat sheet. You'll only be using your fingertips and your brain, and there's nothing wrong with that. Think of it this way: some kids have math heads, and they can figure out all the possible scores that different moves would get them. The ones who are best at Scrabble can do numbers as well as letters. But should they be disqualified because of it?"

"No," said Duncan.

"Correct, Dorfman, correct."

Still, Carl explained, even without the ability to feel tiles or figure out points really fast, there were even more "tricks" you could learn to become a stronger player. Today, sitting on the rug in his bedroom between games, Carl taught Duncan about six-letter bingo stems. These were a combination of six letters which, when scrambled, could have a single letter added to them in order to make a bingo. That single letter could be a blank, Carl said, or it could be one of many different letters of the alphabet.

"Dorfman, listen up. This is a little confusing. The most popular bingo stem is SATINE," Carl said. "If you happen to have these letters on your rack, you can add one of a bunch of *different* letters to them, and then scramble them all up to make a bingo." Carl took out a notebook in which he'd written the letters and words down. They included:

A, which, when added to SATINE, got you the words ENTASIA and TAENIAS

And then:

B, which gave you BASINET and BANTIES.

Going through the alphabet, you could wind up with the following:

C: CINEAST, ACETINS
D: DESTAIN, DETAINS, INSTEAD, SAINTED,
   STAINED
E: ETESIAN
F: FAINEST
G: EASTING, EATINGS, INGATES, INGESTA,
   SEATING, TEASING
H: SHEITAN, STHENIA
I: ISATINE
K: INTAKES
L: ELASTIN, ENTAILS, NAILSET, SALIENT,
   SALTINE, SLAINTE, TENAILS

M: ETAMINS, INMATES, TAMEINS

N: INANEST, STANINE

O: ATONIES

P: PANTIES, PATINES, SAPIENT, SPINATE

R: ANESTRI, ANTSIER, NASTIER, RATINES, RETAINS, RETINAS, RETSINA, STAINER, STEARIN

S: ENTASIS, NASTIES, SEITANS, SESTINA, TANSIES, TISANES

T: INSTATE, SATINET

U: AUNTIES, SINUATE

V: NAIVEST, NATIVES, VAINEST

W: TAWNIES, WANIEST

X: ANTISEX, SEXTAIN

Z: ZANIEST, ZEATINS

Duncan was overwhelmed. "But I don't know most of those words!" he said. "I mean, I know a *few*. Like SALTINE, of course. I've eaten those. Or . . . or . . . SEITANS, which is a vegan thing that my aunt cooks. Or . . . TEASING. I've been teased a lot. But most of them, they're just nonsense to me. Like BANTIES."

"Yep, good old BANTIES," said Carl. "I taught myself to remember that one. Here's how I did it. The word sounds a little like BANTAM, which is a chicken, right?"

"If you say so."

"It is. And it *also* sounds like—this is embarrassing—PANTIES. I know this is going to sound strange," Carl explained, "but, see, I pictured a chicken wearing girls' underpants. And a few months ago, I was playing a game and guess what? I had a blank and SATINE. And I suddenly remembered BANTIES. That little word gave me a ton of points, Dorfman."

With Scrabble, Duncan saw, you didn't need to be a genius. You didn't even have to know what the words meant, though it could be more interesting—and sometimes useful—if you knew the meanings of some of the strange ones. Duncan thought about the word AA, for instance, which he had looked up in the Scrabble dictionary and found out that it meant "rough, cindery lava." If he hadn't known it was a noun, he might have tried to add ING onto the end of it, thinking it was a verb. And, of course, AAING would've probably been knocked right off the board by his opponents.

Or if someone had put down the word FOCI, which happened to be a plural of the noun FOCUS, and Duncan hadn't known it was already plural, he might have tried to add an S to it, making FOCIS, which also would have been knocked off the board.

But as Carl said, it wasn't *necessary* to know what the words meant. You mostly had to know which ones were good, and which ones weren't.

When the games were done, both Duncan and Carl felt restless from sitting for such a long time. "Come on," Carl said, and he grabbed a soccer ball and they ran outside into the Slaters' enormous yard. The wind was like a whip, but they kicked the ball, which was sent smashing by Carl and sent slowly rolling by Duncan. Today, it didn't really seem to matter that Duncan was lousy at soccer. It felt good to be outside in the cold, running around and clearing his head of anagrams and openings and bingo stems. The ball hurtled toward him and somehow Duncan managed to block it with his head, sending it thundering back to where it came from.

"Nice one, Dorfman," Carl had to admit, and Duncan wanted to have a chance to smack another ball back, but Carl's mother waved them inside. It was time for Duncan to leave.

Mrs. Slater drove him to Thriftee Mike's Warehouse, where Duncan's mother was finishing up her workday. Caroline Dorfman had wanted him to meet her there so that Duncan could try on a few more shirts she'd picked out for him. During the ride, Duncan sat beside Mrs. Slater in the black car, which smelled like old smoke and perfume. There was a long, awkward silence, as there often was when you were alone with the parent of a friend.

"So, Duncan," said Mrs. Slater as the car pulled into the parking lot of the superstore. "Be sure to tell your mom that we've got everything taken care of for the big weekend. And also, please tell her I'll be sending her a release form about those ads. We'll need her signature."

"Okay."

"It's going to be a great campaign," she said. "Even though some people have a problem with the product."

"What do you mean?" Duncan asked. "What's the product?"

"Cigarettes."

Duncan stared at her. "Cigarettes?" Had he missed something when she was explaining the photo shoot?

"Yes," she said. "But it's all extremely moral. You see, the company really, really doesn't want kids to smoke. Until they're old enough to make that decision for themselves. It's a personal decision, of course. And we live in a free country."

"I didn't know it was for cigarettes," Duncan said in a faint, queasy voice.

"Oh, I'm sure I mentioned it."

Duncan was becoming surer and surer that she hadn't, but he didn't know what to do. He felt panicky, and he gripped the door handle as though he could simply make a run for it.

"As I'm certain I explained," Mrs. Slater went on, "the ads are for the low-tar cigarette Smooth Moves. You and Carl will be shown playing a game together. And below the photo it will say something about how kids should only participate in wholesome activities. How they shouldn't think about whether they want to smoke until they're fully grown."

It seemed wrong to pose for an ad for cigarettes, Duncan thought, even if the ad said the company was against kids smoking. The company, he knew, was just waiting for today's kids to grow up and become tomorrow's smokers. An alarm went off inside him, telling him this wasn't something he should take part in. It was the same alarm that sometimes rang in him when he thought about using his fingertips during the tournament.

Get out now, he said to himself. *Get out now*. But he couldn't; he didn't know how.

The car pulled up at the entrance of Thriftee Mike's. "Thanks for the lift," Duncan said miserably.

"You're welcome. I'm glad we worked everything out. I think you kids will have a terrific time down in Yakamee. It's only thirteen days from now, isn't that right? So exciting."

Duncan got out of the car and dizzily walked into the store. It was the end of the day, and Thriftee Mike's was almost empty. A man and a woman stood in the huge, brightly lit space examining a lobster-shaped oven mitt they had picked out of a bin. Nearby, a little kid was pawing at a can of Cheezy Chips from another bin. Way across the store, a blond woman in a red smock waved to Duncan. It was his mother.

He walked slowly toward her, wishing he could confess everything. What would his mother possibly say to him? She would be knocked out by all that he revealed. "Cigarettes? Are you serious? And about your power—Duncan, I asked you not to show anyone," she'd say in a heartbroken voice. And then, "You know, if you use your left-hand fingertips that way at the tournament, it will be *cheating*."

"No it won't," he would insist. "Carl told me it won't. There's nothing about fingertips in the rule book."

But he didn't trust Carl Slater's opinion. He didn't trust Carl *or* Carl's mother.

But still Duncan couldn't tell his own mother the truth.

He wasn't sure that he'd be able to convince her it wasn't cheating, and he wasn't sure he could even convince himself. Now, on top of that, Duncan had to convince himself that it was okay to pose for an ad for Smooth Moves. There was no way his mother would ever sign that release form. With a sick feeling, he realized he would have to forge her signature.

Duncan would have liked to sit down on one of the lawn chairs that were for sale in aisle four of Thriftee Mike's, and talk to her. Back when they lived in Michigan, it seemed that they talked so much more.

Here she was now, after a long day of work. I'M THRIFTEE CAROLINE was printed on the name tag on her red smock.

After glancing at it for a few seconds, Duncan mentally moved the letters in CAROLINE, and saw that they formed COLINEAR. That was a word he had heard in math class. You didn't only learn Scrabble words by reading dictionaries or word lists or being tutored by a better player. A lot of the words you knew just from living in the world.

Duncan's mother smiled when he walked up to her, though he could see how tired she looked. "How was your day?" she asked. "Everything okay?"

"Fine. You?"

"Oh, not too bad. A customer had a screaming fit in Ladies' Shoes—her head basically spun three hundred sixty degrees—but otherwise it was quiet. Did you have a nice time with Carl?"

"Yes." Duncan hesitated, wanting to tell her what was on his mind. "You know what, Mom?" he said instead. "Guess who lives right down the street from Carl?"

"Who?"

"Thriftee Mike."

"What?" said his mother.

"Yeah, he lives in one of the other mansions in The Inlet. Carl said he's actually not very thrifty at all. Of course, he's never actually met him. The guy apparently doesn't come out of his house a lot, except when he goes to the store at night."

Duncan's mother's mouth was tight, and she didn't say a word. Duncan realized he probably shouldn't have said something even slightly negative about the owner of the store while they were *in* the store. Maybe none of the employees ever talked about Thriftee Mike. Maybe it was forbidden. He was sorry he had brought it up.

Chimes sounded over the loudspeakers, and a voice announced, "Thriftee Mike's will be closing in fifteen minutes. Please bring all your *thriftee* purchases up to the register."

"We'd better make it snappy," his mother said. "I picked out some nice shirts. They're just like the mustard-yellow one I bought you, but in different colors. One is the color of ketchup, and the other one's like relish. It could be a set." Duncan rolled his eyes.

She motioned toward the nearest counter, which had a dumb sign over it that read, THIS COUNTER IS FOR CUSTOMERS WITH UNDER THRIFTEEN PURCHASES.

Thrifteen?

But this wasn't the time to complain about his shirt, or make fun of the "word" *thrifteen*. This was the time—if he was a much braver person, which he wasn't—to say: Mom, I have to tell you something. I know you'll be mad, but I told everyone in school about my fingertips even though you warned me that something bad would happen. And now

I'm supposed to use them at the tournament on December twelfth, which is basically cheating.

And by the way, the whole trip costs eight hundred and eighty-five dollars, but don't worry, because I'm going to pay for it by posing for a cigarette ad.

Oh, and I'm planning on forging your signature on the release form.

Mom, Duncan wanted to say, that bad thing you warned me about seems to be happening.

But even so, Mom, I'm going to the tournament, I'm *really going*. And even though I'm dreading it in many ways, I also have to tell you this: I am so excited I am jumping out of my skin.

PART TWO

Chapter Nine

DECEMBER 12th

Welcome to the Grand Imperial Hotel, the finest hotel in all of Yakamee," said the friendly woman behind the desk in the marble lobby. "How may I help you? Wait, don't tell me! Y'all are here for the Scrabble thingy."

"Yes, in fact we are," said Caroline Dorfman.

"You and everyone else in this place," said the woman.

The big hotel lobby was packed with people. Many of them were kids, and many held Scrabble sets under their arms, or wore T-shirts that said the name of their Scrabble team. Most were headed toward the escalator, where a sign read: YST ON MEZZANINE LEVEL, with an arrow pointing up. Everyone's voices were loud, because there was a rushing waterfall in the lobby, and a man in a white tuxedo playing a white piano.

But mostly they were loud because December twelfth had finally arrived.

"The reservation is under Dorfman," said Duncan's mother. "If possible, we'd love to check into our room right away and go take a little rest."

"Are you *serious*, Mom?" said Duncan. "We don't have time. Registration is going to close at one!"

Many of the players traveling by car, bus, or train had arrived the night before, but the Drilling Falls team had taken a plane at the crack of dawn that had gotten them here with little time to spare.

"Now, let me see, Ms. Dorfman," said the woman behind the desk. "I can give you a nice classic regular with two queen-sized beds on twenty-three. Although, *hmmm...*" She scrunched up her mouth as she looked at her computer monitor. "It says here that this guest room is by the ice machine. And maybe y'all don't want the buckety sound of *thunk-thunk-thunk* disturbing your sleep at night."

"That's very thoughtful of you," said Duncan's mother. "My son will need his sleep for the tournament."

"I wonder why everybody makes ice cubes *round* these

days," said the woman. "A few years back, the ice people just up and changed the standard shape."

"You know, that's true," said Duncan's mother. "I never thought about it before."

The ice people? There was no time to discuss this boring subject right now, Duncan thought. But the two women looked as if they were settling in to discuss something deep and urgent, like global warming. He would have to put a stop to it.

"Mom," hissed Duncan. "I have to go find Carl and register!"

The Dorfmans had flown with Carl and his mother early this morning, though the Slaters had sat in first class, where they were handed rolled-up warm washcloths, and served omelets from a cart with a little flame that cooked them. As soon as they all arrived at the hotel in Florida, where the Slaters rushed through some kind of VIP check-in, Mrs. Slater had gone upstairs. Carl had slipped away, warning Duncan to hurry up and meet him at the registration table "ASAP," and Duncan saw him step onto the escalator, heading up to the mezzanine.

"Oh, all right," said Duncan's mother, blinking at Duncan as if she'd almost forgotten he was the reason they'd come here in the first place. "You go on. I'll catch up with you in a little while."

He couldn't believe she was letting him go off on his own; she almost never let him do that. Duncan walked quickly away from the front desk. He got on the escalator and rose up toward the roar of other kids, and the sound of tiles being shaken in their bags, and whatever else awaited him this weekend.

Right behind Duncan Dorfman, a gloomy-looking boy with long dark hair and a skateboard stepped onto the escalator. Someone who appeared to be his father stood beside him. Behind them was another man, along with a woman holding a baby girl. The father had one of those beards that you could hide objects in, if he were in a "Find the Hidden Pictures" puzzle. A spoon could be hidden in his beard, and a cricket.

"So the big day has come," the father was saying. "Are you excited, kid?"

"Oh, sure, Dad," said his son. "Thrilled to death."

Although he didn't want to show it, Nate Saviano actually was a little excited. For most of the plane ride down from New York first thing this morning, he'd been in a horrible mood. He had traveled here with his father, his mother, Dr. Steve, and baby Eloise. They'd taken up all the seats in row fourteen except one; some poor lady had to sit directly in the line of smell-fire from Eloise's diaper. Maxie Roth, who incredibly enough had agreed to be his partner, had taken the bus down yesterday with her parents, and was already here, somewhere. Nate had to find her right away. He and Maxie had played a few games together since he'd invited her to be his partner, but all the pressure was on Nate to win the games for them. Maxie knew she was just a seat-filler, though Nate thought she was an extremely cool one.

During the trip his father had wanted him to look over some word lists "just for the heck of it," but Nate shook his head no, and instead he'd watched the tiny TV screen at his seat. He'd even watched the video of the safety demonstration, in which oxygen masks dropped down from above the seats, and all the passengers in the video calmly reached for them, as though getting glasses from a kitchen cabinet.

Then Nate watched some dumb show on the little kids' channel. That terrible kiddie singer Kazoo Stu came on, singing his big hit about wanting someone to take the kangaroo out of his hair. To spite his father, Nate even watched it a *second* time. By late tomorrow afternoon, this period of his life would be over forever, and he'd never have to form the words KEF or OORIE or QANAT again.

But now that he was here at the hotel in Yakamee, Nate had to admit he was impressed by the number of Scrabble players around him. Since Nate had started being homeschooled this fall, he had rarely been around large groups of kids. As the escalator rose to the mezzanine, Nate took in the size of the crowd, and he was amazed.

There were many, many kinds of kids, all of them in motion. What they had in common was Scrabble.

"Whoa," said Nate to his parents as they all stepped off the escalator.

They walked out into the atrium, which was jumping with players. Palm trees actually grew indoors here; the scene was wild. A woman with a clipboard came over and said, "Have you registered?" Nate shook his head no. "Better hurry, then," she said. "You're among the last of them." Maxie Roth was waiting for him by the table with her own parents. Her hair was magenta with a new skunky white streak through it. She held her own skateboard under her arm. When she saw Nate, she flashed him a peace sign, and he flashed one right back.

Someone took a picture of Nate and Maxie, then slapped name tags onto their shirts. They were team #64, the Big Apple Duo—a boring name, Nate thought, but they hadn't been able to come up with anything better.

"Your partner, Maxie, is certainly very *alternative* looking," Nate's mother said after the picture was taken. "And neither of you smiled. It looked like a mug shot! Those boys over there are smiling," said his mother, nodding toward a team that was having its own picture taken. They were called the Surfer Dudes, Nate would find out later. They both wore Hawaiian shirts and shark's-tooth necklaces, and had golden blond hair that looked a little greenish. They were massively big, and their smiles glinted. They were smiling as if they owned the world and all its oceans and landmasses.

"I didn't feel like smiling," he told his mother.

"Well, even so," said Larry Saviano. "You want to look nice, Nate."

"I do?"

"Of course, wise guy," said Dr. Steve. "If you win, they'll put your picture in the paper."

"*If* they win?" said Nate's father. "You mean *when* they win."

"Way to keep up the pressure, Larry," Nate's mother said to her ex-husband. "Way to turn your son into a basket case."

His parents glared at each other the way they always used to when they were married and had an argument, and Nate felt his stomach get tight.

"I just want him to have fun," Larry Saviano murmured, but Nate knew this wasn't entirely true. His father had everything resting on Nate and Maxie winning the championship.

"PAIRINGS!" a man shouted, and approximately two hundred kids swiveled their heads in his direction.

"'Bearings?' What's that mean?" asked Dr. Steve.

"Pairings," said Larry. "It means they've posted the teams that will be playing together for the first round."

All the kids in the atrium swarmed toward the bulletin boards that had been set up by the doors of Ballroom A, where the games would be held. Nate found himself wedged between a slightly chunky, wavy-haired, nervous-looking boy and a small redheaded girl.

He got a good view of the pairings sheet, and he traced downward with his finger until he located his team. "There we are," Nate said to Maxie. "We're playing team number eighty-eight, the Evangelical Scrabblers from Butterman, Georgia."

There would be three rounds packed into today, then a tournament-wide trip to the amusement park Funswamp tonight, then three rounds tomorrow, plus the final round between the two top teams that all the other players would watch live on a movie-theater-size screen, and which would simultaneously appear on *Thwap!* TV. Nate and Maxie were turning to go back to his family when the redheaded girl spoke up.

"Hi," she said. "I'm April." She pointed to her name tag, which read: APRIL BLUNT, TEAM #41, THE OREGONZOS. PORT-LAND, OR.

"I'm Nate."

"Hey. I'm Lucy," said her partner, who had just joined

them. She was a tall black girl with springing dreadlocks. Then Lucy said to April, *"So?"*

"So nothing," said April. "It's not him."

"Not who?" asked Nate.

"Nothing. Not important," April said. Then she said, "Nate, can I ask you something? Who taught you to play Scrabble?"

"My dad did," he said. "He was a Scrabble player when he was my age. He played in this tournament."

"Oh, wow. Well, that's that."

"That's what?" asked Nate.

"Sorry, never mind," said April. "I just wanted to make sure you weren't somebody I once knew. But I didn't really think you were."

"Whatever," said Nate. They wished each other good luck in their games and said they'd see each other later.

As Nate and Maxie walked away, April told her partner, "I didn't really think it was him. I wanted it to be him, I guess."

"What about that one?" asked Lucy, pointing toward the boy with the wavy brown hair and a T-shirt that read: DRILLING FALLS SCRABBLE TEAM. The boy looked a little clueless and lost.

"Oh, it's pretty unlikely that that's him," said April. "But he looks nice," she added.

"Let's say hi, then," said Lucy.

"Okay, sure."

"He looks like he could use a hi." They walked over and introduced themselves. "We're April and Lucy from Portland, Oregon," Lucy announced, and the boy seemed startled to be spoken to by them.

"I'm Duncan. From Drilling Falls, Pennsylvania," he added after a moment, as if he weren't happy about this fact.

"Nice to meet you, Duncan," said April. "Who are you playing first?"

"A team called the Tile Hustlers, from somewhere in Maine."

"Hope you know how to hustle them back," said Lucy. "Are you very experienced?"

"Experienced?" Duncan felt like an impostor here, even though he had improved so much since he'd begun, and now loved the game. Still, it was strange to be wearing one of the T-shirts that Carl Slater's mother had had specially made. She'd given it to Duncan recently, on the day he'd spent at the Slater house unhappily posing for photographs of himself and Carl playing Scrabble for the Smooth Moves cigarette ad.

An unfriendly young woman had come up to Duncan in the Slater living room that day with a makeup kit in her hand. "You need color," she'd said. "You look like death. No offense."

Before he could respond, she'd started brushing powder all over his face. He'd opened his mouth to object, but some of the powder got sucked inside, as if he was in a sandstorm. The whole day had made Duncan feel horrible, including the moment when he'd had to hand in the release form on which he'd forged his mother's signature. He'd carefully written:

Caroline Dorfman

No one even bothered to check whether or not it looked real. Mrs. Slater didn't seem to care.

Duncan had asked Carl to tell his mother not to bring any of this up—the ad, the release form, or the money—to Duncan's mother over the weekend in Yakamee. "She's really sensitive," he'd said vaguely, and Carl had said not to worry, his mom wouldn't say a word.

Maybe, Duncan thought, the ads would never appear anywhere, and he would never have to tell his mother what he'd done. She still thought the trip had been paid for by the school. Not only that, but she still had no idea of the real reason Duncan had been invited to participate. She knew what the fingertips of his left hand could do, but she didn't know that anyone else knew. To Duncan's relief, none of this information had made its way back to her over the fall.

"I'm not experienced at all," Duncan admitted to the girls at the tournament now.

"Well, I'm glad to hear it," said Lucy. "In case we end up playing each other today, I mean. But I bet you're good."

"I don't know about that. How about you two?" he asked.

"We've been playing for a while, but this is our first tournament. We mostly just like the game," said Lucy, but Duncan knew she was probably being modest. He had a feeling the two of them were extremely good.

"I like your T-shirt," April said to him. Then she casually asked, "Do you have a lot of shirts with things written on them?"

"No, just a couple," said Duncan. "I mostly wear regular shirts. My mom brings them home from the store where she works. Unfortunately," he added.

"Why unfortunately?"

"They're the exact colors of mustard, ketchup, and relish."

"Oh. That's not good. But you could be a walking ad for a barbecue," said Lucy.

"I'm already a walking ad for cigarettes," Duncan muttered.

"What?" said Lucy, but Duncan said it was nothing, just a joke, never mind.

"I'm pretty sure the answer to this is no," April said,

"and I know it's going to sound completely weird, but I have to ask you a question: Did you ever own a T-shirt that said 'SETTLE MARS'?"

"No," said Duncan. "Why?"

"Long story," said Lucy Woolery. "But basically, April met someone years ago at a motel pool. He was wearing a T-shirt that said SETTLE MARS. Anyway, you're not the boy from the pool, I assume. You don't have food allergies, like he did, do you? You never met my friend April before. You would probably remember if you had."

"No, I don't have food allergies," said Duncan. "And I've never met your friend. I'm not that boy."

He thought about how he had never been to a motel with a pool before, let alone a big fancy hotel with a pool on the roof, like this one. But still, he thought it was pretty great that he was here now. He lightly curled the fingers of his left hand, then flexed them. In the distance, Duncan could see his mother coming up the escalator, waving to him as soon as she picked him out of the crowd. He waved back.

Suddenly the tall doors of the ballroom were flung open from inside. "IT'S STARTING!" someone shouted, and everyone rushed through the doorway.

Duncan Dorfman, April Blunt, and Nate Saviano went in with the crowd, feeling themselves pushed into the enormous red-and-gold hotel ballroom. Row after row of tables were set up there, each one with a Scrabble game lying on it. Everyone went searching for their tables.

Nate Saviano's father Larry stood for a moment just inside the doorway, looking around in wonder. "I remember this place like it was yesterday," he said to no one in particular, for Nate had already gone deep inside.

A voice came over the loudspeaker. "Attention, players," it said. "Welcome to the tournament. Everyone please find your tables and take your seats. Round one is about to begin."

Chapter Ten
22 MINUTES ON THE CLOCK

The ballroom went dead silent. Duncan Dorfman, his heart wild in his chest, sat beside Carl and across the table from the Tile Hustlers. They did not look like hustlers at all, but still Duncan felt as if he were going to die. What was he doing at a major Scrabble tournament? He didn't belong here.

Duncan shifted in his seat and something rustled in his back pocket. He reached in and pulled out a folded piece of looseleaf paper, having no idea how it had gotten there. Oh no, he thought, my mom put a humiliating note in my pants. It would be covered with hearts and would say something corny like, *I LOVE YOU SO MUCH, DUNCAN, AND NO MATTER WHETHER YOU WIN OR LOSE, YOU ARE "TILE-RIFIC." XOXOXO MOM*

Duncan unfolded the note and saw that he was wrong. It was a note with doodles of space aliens all over the top—the same kind of cartoons that Andrew Tanizaki always drew. He read it to himself:

Hey, Duncan,
Here is a good-luck drawing. I made one for my brother when his appendix burst from a pencil in his pocket, and he survived.
I hope you do really well in the turnoment.
Andrew T.

"What's that?" asked Carl.

"Nothing."

"*'Turnoment?'*" said Carl, reading over Duncan's shoulder. "Oh, right, the Chinaman. He made you a sweet little drawing. Awww," he said in a sarcastic voice.

Duncan carefully placed the note back in his pocket. He felt a little guilty that Andrew, who he no longer sat with at lunch, had given this to him. But he also felt pleased that he had. Though Duncan was nervous as he waited for the game to begin, he realized he would have felt even worse if he hadn't had Andrew's good-luck drawing.

The room was completely hushed now, all the kids focused and alert. Some of them, like Duncan, felt their hearts thumping in their chests.

"We are about to start," said the director of the YST, a slightly red-faced, earnest man named Dave Hopper, speaking into a microphone. "Are there any final questions?"

Everyone looked around the ballroom. No, there were no questions.

But then, oh wait, wait, how annoying, there *was* a question. Just when you thought everyone had silently agreed *not* to ask questions, someone always ruined it. A boy's hand had shot up from the corner. He looked very young, and he and his teammate, a girl, wore matching cowboy hats.

"What if you have to urinate?" the boy asked.

Some kids laughed, and someone else shouted out, "URINATE is an anagram of TAURINE!" but the director took the question seriously.

"I'm glad you asked that," he said. "The answer is in the official rules, which I hope you've all read. But just to remind you: If a player has to go to the bathroom, the other teammate may continue playing, but the bathroom-goer must leave after his or her team has played, and before new tiles are drawn."

Now, were there any more questions?

No, it seemed, there were not.

"Well," said the director, "I guess that's it. Good luck, everyone. Draw your first tiles."

At each of the fifty tables, a player picked up a little tile bag, held it up high, and with the other hand reached inside and blindly swirled the letters around to pick a tile. The player then handed the bag to one of his or her opponents, who selected a tile, too.

At Duncan and Carl's table, Carl drew a P. He handed the bag back to the Tile Hustlers, and the boy with freckles bursting all over his face drew an M. This meant that the Tile Hustlers would go first, since their letter was closest to A. The P and the M were returned to the bag. Duncan gave it a hard shake and placed it on the table. As soon as one of his opponents picked the first tile and looked at it, Duncan slapped his hand down on the button of the electronic timer. It made a *pock* sound, and the clock began counting down from twenty-two minutes.

All around the room came other *pocks*. There was very little talking anymore. Parents and family members sat behind velvet ropes along the sides of the ballroom, or they waited out in the atrium, where you could actually talk without someone angrily saying *"Shhh,"* like a murderous librarian.

Duncan held his breath as he drew all seven tiles in one big scoop. He and Carl had decided that, for the first turn, Duncan would simply draw tiles the regular way. He had gotten Carl to agree that he would keep pulling tiles like that until it became necessary to use his fingertips. Exhaling slowly now, he looked at the letters as he placed them on the rack. He had picked:

M

O

I

S

O

E

R

Together they looked like:

MOISOER

At first glance, it didn't seem to be a great rack. There were certainly some interesting words that could be made from these letters: ISOMER, MOROSE, and even ROMEOS. But it would be a waste to use the S in any of those words. Duncan realized that if the Tile Hustlers played a word with a T in it—a common letter, there were six in each game—he and Carl would be able to make the eight-letter word ROOMIEST. Duncan scribbled a note to Carl, telling him this, and Carl squinted in understanding and nodded.

Duncan and Carl watched the board to see what the other team would do. Please let there be a T in their word, Duncan thought. Please let there be a T. Then we can start the game with a bingo.

The boy without the freckles began to lay down tiles. But when he was done, Duncan and Carl saw that he had placed the word DREAM. There wasn't a single T among its letters. Too bad, Duncan thought. He and Carl had no good options now.

But Carl sat up straight. He took the pad and scribbled something on it, then pushed it toward Duncan, who read:

You're not going to BELIEVE what we missed!
Like, DUH!

Carl Slater began picking tiles up off the rack. You were always supposed to discuss a move with your partner before you played it; you weren't supposed to simply plunk down tiles wherever you liked. Duncan didn't like that Carl was doing this, but then he saw what Carl had played, and he didn't mind at all. Right under the AM in DREAM, Carl had placed the R and an O, making the tiny words AR and MO. Then he kept laying down letters horizontally. OMIES, he played. His word was:

ROOMIES

It was simple slang for "roommates," and Duncan and Carl had become so focused on getting that T for ROOMIEST, that they'd almost missed what was right in front of them. Their opening move was worth a huge 69 points: 19 for ROOMIES, AR, and MO, plus a 50-point bonus for using all their letters. Carl hit the timer.

"Nice," the freckled Tile Hustler said quietly.

"Thanks," said Carl.

From then on, the game was played at a rapid pace. Back and forth the two teams went, laying down their tiles, writing down scores, hitting the timer. A few moves later, their opponents ended up putting a T at the end of ROOMIES to make ROOMIEST after all. They kept going, using an A already on the board for the word OAR, until they had played the bingo DECORATE.

"Wow, great," said Duncan.

"Thank you," said the boy who'd laid the tiles down.

A girl at the adjoining table said, *"Shhhhhhh!"* There was a rule in Scrabble that you were supposed to talk as little as possible during games, which was why players wrote notes to each other. There was even a word for talking too much:

"coffeehousing." But once in a while you ignored the rules and coffeehoused anyway.

Behind the velvet rope at the side of the ballroom, a bald guy in dark glasses turned around to face Nate's half-sister, Eloise, who had been sitting in her mother's lap, making razzberry sounds with her lips, spit flying.

"Excuse me," he said to Nate's mother. "I'd really appreciate it if you could keep your baby under control. The back of my head feels like it's on an ocean voyage. Plus, I'm trying to pay attention."

"I'm sorry," Nate's mother said.

Another mother, a small Indian woman in a pink sari sitting beside the man, turned to him and politely asked, "Which is your team?"

The bald man seemed surprised by the question. "My team?" he said. "They're . . . over there. Excuse me," he said. Then he slipped out of the ballroom and into the atrium.

The two mothers watched him go.

"Strange man," murmured the mother in the sari.

Nate's mother nodded. "I think we should keep an eye on him."

"Rachel," said Dr. Steve to his wife. "Look at Nate; he's smiling! His team must be doing well. That'll make Larry happy."

But Nate's father Larry Saviano wasn't watching. He

had said he was too worried to stay behind the velvet rope, so throughout the first game he had been pacing the edges of the ballroom, glancing all around him. Right now he was on the other side of the room.

Nate, actually, wasn't smiling at all. His mouth was pulled into a tight line that from a distance might have looked like a smile, but wasn't. Nate had quickly realized that his opponents, the Evangelical Scrabblers—a brother and sister, Kaylie and Josh—were a strong team. Right before the game began, the Evangelical Scrabblers had stood beside the table holding hands and looking upward, their mouths moving in silent prayer. Nate and Maxie had watched, surprised. Nate knew it wasn't the chandelier they were looking at, or even the ceiling.

Kaylie had picked a B to start, while Maxie picked an L.

Nate banged down on the clock button to start the other team's timer, and right away the Evangelical Scrabblers moved their tiles around on their rack and busied themselves writing notes to each other. Within seconds, they had put down the word WINDOW, for 34 points.

"WINDOW," Kaylie joked in her Southern accent. "My favorite opening."

Maxie looked at her blankly. "What?" she said.

"It's a pun," Josh said in a similar accent. "A Scrabble pun. Get it? A window is an opening. And, see, this is our *opening* move."

"Ohhhhh," said Maxie, smiling. "I get it."

Then both teams fell silent, concentrating hard. Maxie fiddled with her multiple ear studs. The game, as it turned out, was balanced in terms of the quality of tiles. But then near the end, the Evangelical Scrabblers played FIFE, and the first F landed on a triple-letter square that counted both across and down. The turn was worth a solid 31 points. The Big Apple Duo suddenly fell behind.

Sweat popped out all over Nate's neck, and he told himself: *Think, think!* He and Maxie moved their tiles around on the rack, but time was passing. Nate began to see that unless something good happened fast, the game would be lost.

Their rack, unfortunately, looked like this:

ALALAIN

Maxie moved the tiles around again. But what turned up was:

INALALA

and then . . .

LILNAAA

The tiles were rotten, and they didn't combine well with any of the letters that were already on the board. There was nothing to do, Nate understood, except dump as many of them as they could. All these tiles were one-pointers.

We can't possibly do anything even CLOSE to 31 points, Maxie scribbled on the pad. I see one move for 5,

134

and another that would give us 14, but would also open up the triple. She was very fast with the numbers part of the game—faster even than Nate was. She did mental math at lightning speed, and it was coming in handy. If they traded some or all of their letters now, they would lose their turn and fall even farther behind.

They discussed it briefly, then put down LAIN, which gave them those 5 pathetic points.

Maxie wrote on the pad:

We are, like, doomed.

Nate couldn't believe this was happening in their very first game. He had been working so hard for months, and everything had been building up to this day. What if it all came crashing down? What would his father say?

But in the next hand, the Big Apple Duo picked the X—a letter that everyone always wanted—and they placed it on a triple-letter square going in two directions, making the words XU and XI and earning a whopping 50 points.

Was it possible that they might win the game after all?

Yes, it was possible, and then it actually happened. New York beat Georgia by one point. *One point.*

Nate and Maxie shook hands with the Evangelical Scrabblers, then Maxie said to Nate, "Nice work," and held up her hand for him to slap.

Wearily, he slapped his against it. He liked being with

her, and the two of them were going to try to ride their skateboards while in Yakamee, but he hadn't yet told her how he really felt about the game, or why he was even here. Nate turned away, a little bit dizzy.

"What's the matter?" Maxie asked, but he didn't answer. Yes, they had won, but not by enough. Though he didn't even *like* Scrabble, he knew he had to get his father off his case. Winning games by such a narrow margin was not the way to do that.

"Nate," he heard his father's voice say from across the ballroom.

"*Shhh,*" several parents warned.

"Nate!" called his father again, more urgently.

Maxie looked at Nate and said, "I think your dad wants you."

"Yeah, well, my dad can wait."

"What's going on with you, Nate?" asked Maxie. "You invited me down here, and you seem so . . . angry or something."

"*Shhh,*" warned the parents again. "Games are still in progress!"

"I'll explain later," he said.

Nate turned and saw his father standing in the doorway. Nate nodded and walked toward him, but kept on walking when he reached him. There was a snack stand in the middle of the atrium, and Nate bought himself a can of grape Splurge, tipping his head back to drink.

His father hung over him.

"So what happened?" Larry asked.

Nate stopped drinking and looked at him. "What would you say if I told you we lost?"

Larry's face darkened. *"What?"* he said sharply.

Nate shook his head slowly. "You're incredible, Dad," he said. In that moment he had seen what it would be like if they actually did lose a game. "I was kidding," Nate said. "Maxie and I won."

"You knucklehead! How could you mess with my mind like that? From the way you looked, I thought you actually lost!" Larry's face had now broken into a big smile. "Let's see the score sheet," he said. He took the piece of paper from Nate and examined it carefully. After a moment he glanced up in disbelief. "A *one-point* win?" he said. "Are you serious, Nate? Don't you think that's a little close for comfort?"

"It's a win, Dad," said Nate. "That's what matters."

"Well, that's mostly true," said his father. "*If* you win all your games. If you lose one, your only chance to win is a big spread. You almost blew it here, Nate; can't you see that? You've just got to play better next game, okay? You've just got to push yourself a little harder."

"I played my hardest," said Nate.

His father swallowed, trying to calm down. "I know you did. That wasn't what I meant to say. All I meant is . . ."

". . . 'Just don't let it happen again,'" said Nate.

Nate's father laughed uncomfortably. "Yeah. Something like that," he said.

They understood each other perfectly.

All around the ballroom, the first games were finishing up. Some players walked out smiling, or with fists pumping the air. "The Word Gurrrls rock!" cried a short, stocky girl who, along with her partner—both of them wearing matching sparkly cat's-eye eyeglasses—laughed happily. Other players walked out slowly, barely looking up from the floor. A boy was sniffling as though he had lost his dog. But most of the players were calm and casual as they walked out. In many cases it was hard to tell if they had won or lost.

April and Lucy came out chatting with their opponents, a boy and a girl from Ohio. All of them seemed to be in a good mood.

Duncan and Carl had beaten the Tile Hustlers by 96 points. After the two teams had traded those early bingos, the Drilling Falls team had picked what was left of all the good letters throughout the game. Carl was practically rocking back and forth on his heels now that the game was over, thrilled that he'd drafted Duncan Dorfman to be his partner this year. Poor Brian Kalb had been left in the dust. With Duncan's fingertip talent, Carl was surely thinking, they were going to go all the way.

Carl pulled Duncan over to the side of the atrium, beneath a palm tree. "Dorfman, I want to buy you a soda," he said. "Any flavor you want. And I'll even throw in a straw for free. You did a great job in there," Carl went on. "Your fingertips are awesome, and you're so subtle about it. You're on *fire,* man. Slap me five. With the left, obviously."

Carl held up his hand, and Duncan awkwardly held up his own hand and lightly thudded it against Carl's. "Ow-*oooh,*" Carl howled, as though the heat of Duncan's hand had burned his own.

Duncan didn't know how to tell Carl this, but he hadn't used his power to draw any of those tiles from the bag. He hadn't needed to. Duncan had simply drawn good tiles by chance. You never knew what kind of letters you would get in a game of Scrabble. Sometimes they were terrible, but sometimes, if you were lucky, they were great.

Before the weekend, Carl had reluctantly accepted that Duncan would use his fingertips during the tournament as little as possible. But Drilling Falls's tiles in this first game had been so good that Carl had *assumed* that Duncan had deliberately picked them.

Now, standing in the atrium after the game, Duncan

made a silent promise to himself that he wasn't going to use his fingertips unless it was an absolute *emergency*. He wouldn't use them unless he and Carl were basically on the Scrabble equivalent of the *Titanic*, sinking fast. Otherwise, it would be cheating.

Besides, Duncan liked not knowing which letters would appear on his rack. He even liked experiencing the misery that hit you when your letters were horrible, or the excited feeling you got when they all came together in several good combinations, or in one astonishing, knock-it-out-of-the-park bingo.

Duncan wanted to play the game the way everyone else did. He had been brought all the way down here because of his fingertips, but he had played the first game like a regular player. Selfishly, he didn't want to give that up. He was about to explain all this to Carl, but then he stopped himself, sensing that Carl would be furious. Maybe it was better to keep it to himself. After all, they had won the first game. This was supposed to be a *happy* moment.

"Thanks," was all Duncan said.

By now, all the games were finished, and the players were on a break. Some of them rode the escalators up and down, and one boy was climbing up the down escalator.

Nate Saviano, standing unhappily by the snack stand with his father, said, "I'll see you later, Dad." Then he went over to the big glass wall and sat down on the floor, looking out at the day. Outside, non-Scrabble people walked by in shorts and bathing suits. Cars went past with surfboards strapped to their roofs. This was Florida, but the sunshine and the ocean seemed far away.

From across the atrium, the bald guy with dark glasses stood and watched Nate. Behind his shades, he narrowed his eyes.

Chapter Eleven
WHY ARE YOU HERE?

That man is totally staring at Nate," April whispered to Duncan and Carl during the break.

"Who's Nate?" Duncan asked.

"The cool kid with the long hair and the skateboard. The one from New York," said Lucy.

"Maybe it's his dad," Carl said.

"No. I saw him with his dad earlier," April said. "His dad has a beard. This is someone else."

"Maybe it's his bodyguard," Carl said.

"That's ridiculous. And anyway, bodyguards usually

have earpieces so they can talk to each other," said Lucy. "This guy has no earpiece. He isn't protecting Nate, I'm sure of that."

They all looked across the room at the bald man with dark glasses. "You know, you really can't be sure that he's even watching Nate," said Duncan. "Maybe his eyes are closed. Maybe he's asleep standing up."

"Asleep standing up?" said Lucy. "Is that physically possible?"

"It's rare," said Carl, "but it happens. I saw something about it on *Freaks of Science*, on the Learners' Channel."

"We should tell Nate to be on the lookout for a creep," April said.

Why would a man in dark glasses stare at a kid at a Scrabble tournament unless he was a threatening person? There had to be other explanations, but April couldn't think of any right now. She and Lucy, along with Duncan and Carl, approached Nate and told him their suspicions.

"Staring at me? Where?" said Nate, looking around the atrium.

"Over there," said Duncan, tipping his chin.

"Don't look at him right now, Nate," Lucy warned. "It'll be too obvious. Only look at him when he's looking away."

"How about now?" Nate asked. "Can I look now?"

"Oh, wait," said April. "Too late! While we were talking, he just left."

In that moment, the bald guy had slipped out of the atrium and pushed through the fire doors, and Nate didn't get a chance to see what he looked like. "You were all probably imagining things," Nate Saviano said. "But thanks for looking out for me."

Soon a gong was struck, which meant that round two was about to start. The three teams agreed to meet up afterward and have a quick snack together on the patio. "Whoever gets there first," said April, "grab a big table."

April and Lucy found themselves playing their second game against two brothers from Idaho. Although the Spuds took an early lead, April and Lucy eroded it bit by bit, and ended up winning.

Nate and Maxie played their second game well, too, though so did their opponents. Near the end, the opposition from Missouri fell badly behind. When it was over, they all shook hands across the board. The game had been completed quickly, and the ballroom was still quiet and vibrating with concentration. Nate and Maxie went out into the atrium to find their parents and tell them the outcome.

Larry Saviano was pacing in circles around the snack stand. When he saw Nate he snapped to attention like a dog that's heard its master's car pull into the driveway. "Well?" he said. "No jokes this time. My heart can't take it."

"We *won!*" Nate yelled into his father's face, part resentful, part excited.

His father threw his arms around him. "I knew you could do it," Larry said. "You're on your way, kid."

Inside the ballroom at table eight, Duncan Dorfman sat gazing at his tiles. They weren't particularly good letters, he knew. Surely Carl expected that on their next turn, Duncan would use his fingertips to pick something better from the bag. But the thing was, it *still* wasn't necessary.

Duncan and Carl's round two opponents were two tiny kids, a boy and a girl from Wyoming named Tim and Marie. Everyone in the tournament was in fifth through eighth grade, but these kids looked as if they were only in *second* grade. They wore cowboy hats that were too big for their heads, stitched with embroidery that spelled out the name of their team, the Wranglers. Duncan realized Tim was the boy who'd raised his hand before the tournament to ask what would happen if you had to urinate.

Before the game began, the Wranglers kept talking about how excited they were to be here. They could have never afforded to come, they explained. "But our whole town raised money at a bake sale to send us here," said Tim.

Duncan wondered how these kids had been chosen by their town to come to Florida. Wasn't anyone else better at Scrabble? The Wranglers played as though this was one of their first games ever. They kept making phony words, and Duncan didn't even think they were doing it on purpose. It started when they picked up some tiles from their rack and laid down FITO.

Marie said confidently, "FITO. Eleven points." Tim entered it on their score sheet.

Duncan and Carl looked at each other, confused. Duncan scribbled to Carl,

Maybe it's a word we don't know.

Carl wrote:

Maybe. But I bet they think it's how you spell
FIDO, like the dog.

The word hardly seemed worth challenging, since Duncan and Carl weren't completely sure. And it was only worth eleven points, after all.

But then, two turns later, the Wranglers put down SLEFT.

Carl smirked at Duncan. "Hold!" he said. These kids from Wyoming were either bluffing their way through the whole game, or else they didn't know what was real and what wasn't. Duncan felt sorry for them, but Carl wrote him a note that read:

Challenge?

Duncan nodded. "Challenge!" Carl said, pressing the center button on the timer to pause it.

All four players stood, and together they walked over to one of the laptop computers positioned on stands around the edge of the room. The computers were set to a special word-judge program called Syzygy, which, naturally, was a word that was good in Scrabble. SYZYGY, Duncan had learned, meant a situation in which separate things line up and fall into place.

Please let this all fall into place, Duncan thought.

Carl typed in the letters of SLEFT. Marie, making sure that he had typed it correctly, pressed ENTER. All at once a new screen popped up with a red border, along with the words:

NO, THIS PLAY IS NO GOOD

"Oh," said Marie, moving back a little as if shocked by what she saw. "Wow."

"What? It isn't good?" Tim asked.

The little girl shook her head, her mouth trembling. Duncan felt *awful*. It seemed cruel to beat these little kids, but this was the YST, and you were supposed to play your best, right? Marie picked up the S, L, E, F, and T and returned them to the rack. The Wranglers lost a turn. The button on the timer was pressed again, and game play continued.

"We could have played that game in our sleep," Carl boasted a little later when he and Duncan, April, Lucy, Nate, and Maxie sat together out on the hotel patio overlooking the beach. "We could have played that game if we were *dead*. If we were corpses lying in our *graves* we could have beaten those kids. I don't even know what those kids are doing here. They should be back in Wyoming riding their dumb little miniature ponies in a circle."

"Maybe," April said, irritated, "they're here because they like Scrabble."

"They did seem into it," Duncan agreed. "At least until we challenged them." He thought about how the Wranglers had confidently plunked down those words that turned out to be no good.

"I'm not here because I'm into it," Nate said.

"Oh no?" asked Duncan. "Then why?"

"I'm here because of my dad's obsession." He turned to Maxie and said, "Sorry, Maxie, I should've explained this to you back in New York."

"Explained what?"

Nate told everyone what had happened to his father and his father's partner, Wendell Bruno, at the tournament twenty-six years earlier. "See, I've *got* to win," Nate said. "And first place, not second place like my dad and Wendell Bruno. If I don't win the whole enchilada, my dad won't be able to get over it. I'll have to practice again for *next* year's tournament. I'll never be able to go back to school. But please don't let that affect the way any of you play, if you happen to play a game against Maxie and me. I mean, play your hardest," he added.

"Why do you care about going back to school? School's overrated," said Carl. "Listen to how pathetic our school in Drilling Falls is: we eat lunch at ten forty-five A.M. And it's basically dog food."

Duncan thought again about Andrew Tanizaki, and how they no longer sat together in the cafeteria. He remembered the note with the drawings on it that Andrew had slipped into his back pocket, and now it seemed important not to lose it this weekend. Duncan touched his pocket to make sure it was still there. It was.

"That sounds pretty bad," said Maxie. "My school's all right."

"I'll say," said Nate. "I loved it there."

"I wouldn't go as far as *love*," said Maxie. "But," she told everyone, "we do have a skate park across the street."

"Our school," Duncan said, "is filled with kids you'd never want to talk to. Or at least kids who'd never want to talk to *me*."

As soon as he said this, he also thought: *And Carl's one of them.* Carl would never have said two words to Duncan if he hadn't thought Duncan could help him. He was kind of mean, but he wasn't terrible, and they were getting along fine at the tournament. Mrs. Slater hadn't mentioned the eight hundred and eighty-five dollars *or* the cigarette ads. Even Duncan's mother, now that he thought about it, was trying hard not to intrude.

It was as if, for one weekend, they were all allowed to live in a world devoted to their game. When the weekend was over, they would return to the real world, where no one knew what bingo-bango-bongos were, and where vowel dumps sounded like something embarrassing that could happen to you on the toilet.

"I'm here," Maxie Roth said, "because Nate asked me to be his partner. It seemed kind of different. I'm not so great with words, but I'm really into numbers. Like, figuring out all the scores you could get if you made different moves. And what would happen if the other team did one thing versus another."

"You should see how fast Maxie figures these things out," Nate said. "It's awesome. She's even better than me."

April said, "I'm here because I love the game. Also," she added, "because I want to prove to my super-jock family that Scrabble's a sport."

"Well, *is* it a sport, actually?" asked Duncan.

They debated the question. Then Lucy announced

that April was also here for another reason, and April immediately said to her, "Nobody's interested in that."

But Lucy wouldn't stop. She told everyone at the table the whole story about the boy from the motel pool in the blue T-shirt that said SETTLE MARS. She told them about how she and April had searched for him, and how they'd had no luck so far. "April has no idea of who he is or where he lives," Lucy said. "But she taught him to play Scrabble that day, and he was really good. So maybe he's here this weekend."

"Do you have a crush on him, April?" asked Carl. "Do you want him to be your *boyfriend*?"

"*No,*" said April sharply. "As a matter of fact I don't, so just be quiet, okay?"

"I think you have a crush on him," Carl went on. "April loves Mystery Pool Boy, and wants to make out with him!"

"Oh, shut up, Carl," said Lucy. "Seriously. You're such an infant."

"April?" said Maxie. "I don't know anything about Scrabble. And, like, I don't want to make you feel bad. But, statistically, the chances of him being one of the kids at this tournament are, well, totally low."

"I know," said April. "It's just a sort of a daydream of mine."

"SETTLE MARS," said Duncan. "That sounds so weird."

"Maybe he's just a weird kid," Nate Saviano said.

"Maybe his father forces him to stay home from school and study Scrabble all day."

"You aren't weird, Nate," Maxie said, looking at him. "I think you're interesting." Then she glanced around the table, stopping at Duncan. Everyone else had said why they'd come to the YST. Maxie Roth asked, "So what's your story, Duncan?"

He knew he couldn't tell them the truth; if he did, someone might try to get him disqualified from the tournament. But the truth wasn't so simple. He was here not only because of his fingertips, and not only because he wanted to win first place and show everyone at school that he was special and important and more than just a human piece of ordinary nothingness. And not only because he wanted to hand his mother the prize money and make it possible for them to move to their own place. The truth was also that he loved Scrabble now.

"I'm basically here," Duncan told them, "because I want to be."

Lucy popped open a can of lemon-lime Splurge and nodded. "Makes sense," she said.

They still had a little while until they had to go back inside and play round three. Nate and Maxie showed them some moves on their skateboards, and Carl and Lucy tried them. "Can you ollie?" Nate asked, and Carl said sure, he'd done it plenty of times, and Lucy said no, she'd only ridden once or twice, but she hadn't learned much.

"There are a lot of variations on the ollie," Maxie explained to them, getting on her hot pink skateboard and expertly doing a few tricks. On his own skateboard, Nate was also impressive.

One by one, the kids tried the skateboards. All except Duncan, who sat still, watching. Finally Nate came over and handed him his board. "Come on, man," Nate said. "Your turn."

Duncan thought that Nate Saviano had something about him that made him practically another species from Duncan. Nate had his own style, and his very own way of being in the world. No one picked out Nate's shirts for him. Nate had long hair and an intense expression on his face, and all those skateboard buttons on his jacket. But he was nice. And here he was, holding out the skateboard.

"No thanks," Duncan said. "I don't . . . do that."

"It's not so hard," said Nate. "You'll get the hang of it pretty fast."

"It isn't that," said Duncan. But it *was* that. That and more. Duncan had always worried about his nervous mother's reactions to everything he did. He could just picture her poking her head over the railing above the patio and calling, "Duncan! What do you think you're doing? You'll hurt yourself!"

He had held himself back from doing many things

over the twelve years of his life, but it wasn't really because of her. It was because of him. It made him nervous to try something new. And yet if you never tried *anything* new, Duncan thought, then everything was boring. Life was like an eighty-year-long bus ride in the rain.

Duncan stood up and took the skateboard.

"Go for it," said April.

"Way to go, Duncan D," said Maxie.

Duncan put a foot on the skateboard and immediately felt it flip out from under him as if it was alive. "Whoa!" he said, stumbling off and catching his balance.

"Take it easy," said Nate. "Try again."

The others watched as Nate gave Duncan the first skateboard lesson of his life. It was extremely hard; harder than math and gym rolled into one. The board was so small and narrow; how were you expected to stay on it? It was like riding a chopstick. Duncan fell off several times, but he hadn't been going very fast, and the red tile surface of the patio wasn't that far a fall.

The pace of the lesson soon picked up, and all the kids left the table and moved over to a hilly concrete area.

Duncan grabbed the board. He got on it again, wobbling, and went down the concrete slope, and before he knew it he was going too fast. Behind him the other kids' voices called out, "Duncan! Duncan! Where are you going?"

Where *am* I going? Duncan thought in terror. He

was speeding down a hill, heading toward something he couldn't even see. And he was heading there faster than he'd ever gone in his life. Oh my God, oh my God, oh my God, he thought. Miraculously, Duncan stayed on the skateboard. Inside his sneakers, his toes gripped down like claws. He leaned to the left a little, rounding a curve, passing a couple of palm trees and a man selling cups of sweet shaved ice. He passed a surfing shop, and a souvenir stand, and he kept on going, his feet clinging to the board. Sometimes he crouched down a little, though no one had taught him to. It seemed as if his usually clumsy self knew what to do.

"Watch out!" he called. This was *amazing*. Duncan was roaring down the sidewalk, and people were jumping out of the way. *"Ayy-eeeeeee!"* Duncan heard himself yell. And then the board just popped out from under him again, and he flew into the air.

This time, the world was frozen in place. It was very still up there where Duncan hung, and very quiet.

He thought: This is what it's like right before you die.

At least, he thought, I got to do some amazing things before I died. I got to take a joyride on a runaway skateboard. And be in a national Scrabble tournament. And start to make a bunch of new friends. And run around a little, without my mother watching my every move.

But then the world *unfroze*, and Duncan thudded

down to the ground. His knee slammed against concrete, and he heard himself shout out a word that would never be acceptable in school Scrabble. He was definitely hurt, but he definitely wasn't dead. Duncan heard the other kids' voices coming toward him. They sounded out of breath.

"Duncan! Duncan! Are you okay?" Nate asked, kneeling beside him.

Duncan lay on the ground with his knee throbbing like a little heart. At first he was speechless. His mother would be *hysterical*, he thought. He glanced down at his knee. The pants had ripped, and through the flap in the fabric he saw blood, which had started to spread.

"ARE YOU OKAY?" Nate shouted, right in his ear now.

"No, I'm not okay," Duncan said with a moan.

"Can you move it?" Nate asked.

"I don't know."

"Well, try."

Duncan moved it. The knee worked. Nothing was broken. It was a badly banged-up and extremely bloody knee, but it wasn't actually a disaster. There was a difference. His pants had been ruined, and he'd need to get another pair at Thriftee Mike's Warehouse. But the knee would be okay. It would be okay, and so would he. He had ridden a skateboard very fast, too fast, and he'd gone down a hill on the sidewalk, scaring everyone, including himself, but he had survived.

Sometimes you had to take big risks if you wanted something. Everyone else had always known this, but Duncan never had. Now he knew what they had meant. The ride down the hill had been terrifying. Stupid. Really terrifying and really stupid. But also, it had been incredible.

"We'll get you some ice and a bandage," said April. "They've got to have a first-aid kit around here somewhere."

"Yes, Scrabble injuries must be very common," said Lucy. Duncan laughed a little despite the pain, and then they all helped him to his feet.

Chapter Twelve
A REUNION

Nate's father paced the atrium during round three. He was so tense now that he could barely think. Let him win, Larry Saviano thought. Please, please let him win.

Larry tried to imagine what he would say if Nate came out and told him he had lost a game, and if this time he was telling the truth. Larry certainly couldn't shout, "HOW COULD YOU HAVE LET THAT HAPPEN?" You weren't supposed to shout at your kid when he lost a game. You were supposed to say, "You gave it your best shot, buddy," and put your arms around him and take him out for a hot fudge sundae and buy him a golden retriever named

Cody. But Larry didn't really know what he would do if Nate lost.

So it couldn't happen. Nate *had* to win.

Larry Saviano kept pacing the atrium, knowing how agitated he probably looked. The stress of the tournament was really getting to him. Inside the ballroom, Nate's mother and stepfather sat waiting with baby Eloise, among all the other families. Two hundred players hunched over their Scrabble boards in intense, aching silence.

Larry would have kept pacing back and forth for the entire game, but as he walked across the carpeting with the ugly abstract-art swirl design in it for the thirtieth or fortieth time, someone stepped into his path.

It was the bald guy with dark glasses. Larry had seen him around earlier. The two men stood very still now, just looking at each other. There was something familiar about him, Larry thought, but he didn't know what it was.

"Larry?" said the bald guy.

"Yes?"

"Don't you recognize me?"

"I'm afraid I don't," said Nate's father, but as he spoke, the bald guy reached up and lifted his dark glasses. Behind them his eyes were clear and bright blue. Without the shades on, he didn't look menacing at all. He looked young.

And in that moment, Larry Saviano felt as if he had

stood right here in this atrium before, facing this very same person. But how could that be true?

Because it *was* true.

No, it's not possible, he thought.

Nate's father felt slightly dizzy, and his throat went dry and tight. Finally he understood what was happening. In a cautious voice Larry said, "Wendell? Wendell Bruno? Is it really you?"

The other man smiled slightly and nodded. "Yes, it's really me. Your old Scrabble partner."

It had been twenty-six years since these two men had been here together as twelve-year-old boys. Back then, Larry had obviously had no beard, and he hadn't even begun to shave. Wendell had had a full head of frizzy hair then, and no dark glasses shielding his bright blue eyes. They had been good friends and Scrabble partners, but the loss of the game in the final round had devastated them both.

Their friendship became painful, and whenever they got together after Yakamee, all they thought about was losing. So the two boys drifted apart, and then Wendell's family moved away from their town in Arizona, and Larry never saw him again. He had mostly stopped wondering about him. Even *thoughts* of Wendell Bruno had needed to be blotted out.

But here he was, miraculously, after all this time. Unblottable.

"Wendell, what are you doing here? Do you have a kid in the tournament, too?" Nate's father asked.

His former Scrabble partner shook his head. "No," he said. "I just come here to watch every year. I live right in Yakamee."

"You do? That's a coincidence."

"Not really. I moved here years ago. I wanted to live in the place where my loserdom began."

"You moved to Yakamee, Florida, just because we lost the tournament here?" asked Larry.

"I guess you could put it that way," said Wendell. "And besides, the climate is nice. I got myself a job at Funswamp."

"The amusement park? What do you do there?"

"I'm a character."

"What do you mean?"

"Well," said Wendell Bruno, "Funswamp is trying to be competitive with the more well-known amusement parks in the state. So it came up with its own set of characters. You know—the cute, lovable creatures that kids want to meet and shake hands with and hug. I'm the main one: Scaly the Gator."

"Scaly? I'm not sure that's the most appealing name," said Larry.

"Ah, the kids love Scaly. At least I think they do," Wendell added. "I dress up as a big green-and-rust-colored alligator that's the color of certain kinds of algae. And I go up to the kids and I say"—and here Wendell put on a dopey, slowed-down voice—"'I'm Scaly! Would you like to hug me? But be careful, those scales are rough!'"

"Oh," said Larry politely. "I see. You know, maybe I'm wrong. Maybe they do love you, Wendell. Actually, we're going to the amusement park tonight. There's going to be an outing there. All the kids from the tournament are being bused over."

"That would never have happened in the old days," said Wendell.

"Funswamp didn't *exist* in the old days," said Larry. "It was just a swamp crawling with alligators."

"True. I see you've got a son playing," said Wendell. "I saw his name on the roster, and I knew it had to be your kid. Every year when the tournament pulls into town, I look to see if there's a Saviano. I figure that Scrabble talent is at least partly genetic. And this year, what do you know: 'Nate Saviano.'"

"In all honesty, my son Nate would rather be on his skateboard," said his father. "He's really good at it. You should see him."

"Me, I come to the tournament every year just to drink in the atmosphere," said Wendell. "And to remember what it was like back then."

"Oh, come on," said Larry. "Be honest. You come here

every year to torture yourself. To remember how close we came to victory, and how we lost it."

"Yeah, I guess that's pretty accurate," Wendell admitted with a sad little laugh. "We were two kids who had a chance to become winners," he said. "And then we didn't."

"No, we didn't."

"And our lives have been affected because of it. At least, mine has. How's *your* life been, Larry?" Wendell asked. "Loserish or winnerish?"

"It's been a mixed bag," Nate's father said. "I got divorced. But the best thing that ever happened to me was my son. I know I drive Nate crazy. I just can't help myself."

"He's *got* to win the tournament, right?" said Wendell.

Larry nodded. "Yes," he said softly. "It would really mean a lot to me."

"You know, I've been watching your kid since this morning," Wendell Bruno said. "He had a squeaker with the first game, but then things picked up. He's a strong player, Larry. I started thinking that if he and his partner win the whole thing, it would mean a lot to *me* as well. It would be like reliving the past and *fixing* it, you know? Having it end the right way, finally."

"That's exactly how I feel," said Larry Saviano.

"Maybe," said Wendell, coming closer, "I could help make that happen. Can we go somewhere private to talk?"

Nate's father nodded, and followed him onto the up escalator.

One level above, in Ballroom B of the Grand Imperial Hotel, the Junior National Gymnastics Competition was taking place. Some of the gymnasts' parents wandered around the upstairs atrium, which was identical to the one below, but none of the parents looked familiar to Larry. There was no overlap between this world and the world of Scrabble one flight down. He and Wendell could talk freely here.

Out of curiosity, Nate's father opened the door of Ballroom B a crack and peered inside. Gym mats had been rolled out on the floor, and there was a blur of movement. All around the edges of the ballroom, parents sat watching their kids. "Go, Suzy, go! Go, Suzy, go!" a mother and father chanted excitedly. All the young gymnasts had intense expressions on their faces as they performed their elaborate routines.

Larry gently shut the door and the two men went to sit in big armchairs in the adjacent atrium. "Here's the thing," Wendell said quietly. "I've been following the different games today."

Larry nodded. "And?" he said.

Wendell Bruno took a crumpled receipt from a fast-food place out of his pocket. "Here," he said. "I made a list of the teams that pose the greatest threat to Nate and Maxie."

Larry looked down at the receipt for a triple bacon burger and a large Frooty Slurp. Across it Wendell had written:

THE OREGONZOS

THE SURFER DUDES

THE WORD GURRRLS

THE DRILLING FALLS SCRABBLE TEAM

"So how can this list help?" asked Larry. Whatever Wendell was planning, he didn't like the feel of it.

"Just trust me," said Wendell. "Can you do that?"

"I don't know. We haven't seen each other in twenty-six years. That's over a quarter of a century."

"Think what it would be like if Nate won," Wendell said. "Can you picture it? Can you taste it? Can you *imagine* it?"

Nate's father closed his eyes. Yes, he could almost imagine it. He desperately needed to find a way to make his son win, and he would do whatever it took.

Chapter Thirteen

PREPARE TO BE AMUSED

The doors of the ballroom were thrust open and Duncan emerged, limping on his injured knee. He took a deep breath, then slowly let it out. His team had won game three, the last game of the day, although it had been a rough game, and not because of their opponents, but because of Carl. Early in the match, when it was Duncan's turn to draw tiles, he'd picked an N, an E, and an L, which were completely ordinary letters—not disastrous, but not good. Carl, who'd been watching him closely, was shocked that Duncan had picked those tiles. He fiercely wrote on the notepad: FTPS, DORFMAN, FTPS!

Duncan didn't have to be told that FTPS meant "fingertips."

Carl drew three thick lines under the second FTPS.

But Duncan just shook his head no. He had resolved that he wanted to play without any help for as long as he could. Carl was confused, because he believed that Duncan had *already* used his fingertips to help win the first game. So why wasn't he doing it again now? Carl wrote on the pad:

Why not?

And Duncan just wrote back:

Because I don't want to.

Carl didn't realize that the good letters Duncan had picked in the first game had been selected completely by chance, and that the second game, against the Wranglers, had, of course, just been a blowout. But the opponents in game three, the Proud Nerds, were very, very good, and the Drilling Falls team's tiles were not. It became obvious to Carl as the game wore on and the clock ran down that Duncan was not using his fingertips at all. Drilling Falls managed to pull ahead through intense planning and smart moves, and at the end of the game, which Drilling Falls won 391 to 378, Carl pulled Duncan by his arm over to the side of the ballroom, and said, "What were you just doing in there?"

"Playing."

Carl kept his grip on Duncan's arm. "Look, we had a deal, dude. The only reason you're here is because of how you can help the team. We came really close to losing that one. Did you hit your head, too, when you fell off the skateboard? Is that it? I want to see you using your stuff. Do what you're supposed to do."

He sharply released Duncan's arm and walked off, but as Duncan went to tell his mother they'd won, he could still feel the pressure of Carl's grasp.

Duncan's mother was nowhere to be found. She had told him she'd be waiting for him right outside the ballroom after the game, but she wasn't here. He watched as other kids went up to their parents to tell them how their games had gone. He had an uneasy feeling that something was wrong.

Duncan limped to the lobby, and was making his way toward the elevators to go up and check on his mother, when April Blunt tapped him on the shoulder.

"Hey, Duncan, how'd you guys do?"

"We won again. You?"

"We won, too. And I hear that so did Nate and Maxie. It's a good way to end the day. That knee okay? You're limping pretty badly."

"They gave me some ice and some antibacterial stuff," Duncan said. "But it's no big deal." Actually, the knee was still throbbing, but he had other worries.

"Hey, listen," said April, "tonight at Funswamp, maybe we can go on a couple of rides together."

"Sure," he said. "Do you know I've never been to an amusement park?"

"Really? Never? Well, prepare to be amused."

Duncan took the glass elevator upstairs to eighteen and slid the card into the door of his room. The green light popped on, and Duncan pushed the door open and went in. The room was dark and the shades were drawn. In one of the two beds, his mother lay under the covers.

He knew what this meant: she'd had another migraine. MIGRAINE, he thought, is an anagram of IMAGINER. These days he couldn't stop doing that.

"Mom?" Duncan asked. "Are you okay?"

"Oh, hi, honey," she said, opening her eyes. "You're back. How was the game?"

Duncan slowly walked through the room.

"You're *limping*!" she said. Even in the dark she could tell, and she reached out a hand for the light.

"It's nothing," he said quickly. "You don't need to turn on the light. It'll hurt your eyes."

"What happened?" she asked.

"I fell," said Duncan. Which wasn't untrue. "But we won," he added quickly. "Carl and I are undefeated."

"Well, that's wonderful. Congratulations."

"When did the migraine start?" Duncan asked, sitting down on the other bed and elevating his painful knee.

"It came on all of a sudden," she said. "I saw the aura—

you know—and then I got into bed and waited for the headache. And boy, it came. It's been vicious."

"But did something happen first?" Duncan persisted. "Something stressful?"

"No," said his mother. "I was sitting and having a nice conversation with Nate Saviano's dad, Larry."

"What were you talking about?"

"Oh, nothing much. He was saying something about how hard it is to be a single parent. I agreed. We compared notes, and we both said that you kids are terrific. That was all." She paused. "Listen, I don't think I can go to Funswamp," she said. "Will you be okay without me?"

"No problem, Mom," Duncan said.

"If I rest up, I should be all better by tomorrow," she said. "And we can watch the final round together on the big screen. Unless, of course, you're *in* it."

Duncan thought about his mother's conversation with Nate's father. He remembered that once, when he was little, he'd had a bad cough with lots of phlegm. His mother had dragged an air mattress into his room and spent the night on the floor beside his bed. The vaporizer had hissed, and Duncan had coughed and coughed, and he and his mother had told each other knock-knock jokes all night.

He knew he'd missed out on having a father who could also lie on the floor on an air mattress once in a while when you had a bad cough. But if you'd never had something to begin with, then after a while you forgot what you didn't have. If your father had died of panosis before you were born, then you always thought of yourself as someone whose father had died of panosis before you were born. It was just your *story*; it was just part of who you were.

His mother dropped back to sleep now, and Duncan went into the bathroom to change out of his bloody, ripped pants and into a fresh pair. Then he grabbed a sweatshirt from his overnight bag and slipped from the room.

Two flights down, April Blunt sat on the bed she was sharing with her sister Jenna, who was thunking a basketball against the wall. "Don't you think the people in the next room might not like that?" April asked her.

"Might not like what?"

"The basketball hitting the wall sixty times a minute."

"Oh," said Jenna, stopping. "I hadn't realized."

Instead, she began to spin it on her finger. Jenna could never keep still. It was similar to the way April couldn't keep still inside herself now. Something kept knocking against her brain, reminding her how much she wanted to show her family that Scrabble was a sport, an amazing sport. Reminding her how much she wanted them to be interested in her.

But still, though she knew it was crazy, she also wanted to find that boy from the motel pool. He wasn't here at the YST; she was pretty sure of that by now. But maybe, she thought, if she and Lucy won the tournament and their picture appeared in the papers and on the Internet, the boy from the pool would see it, wherever he lived, and a tiny lightbulb would pop on in his brain.

I know that girl, he would say to himself. *We met once. She told me the anagram ROAST MULES, and I never figured it out.*

ROAST MULES, he would think . . . *ROAST MULES . . . I have to get in touch with her.*

But this was a ridiculous, demented fantasy, April knew as she sat on her hotel bed with a basketball spinning near her head. The boy would never reappear.

Three more flights below, Nate Saviano walked down the long hallway with his skateboard under his arm, heading for the vending machine. His earbuds were in his ears, and he was listening to his favorite band, The Lungs.

Nate wished he could get on his board now and skate forever, and never have to think about anything else. He pictured himself and Maxie Roth doing ollies and heelflips while yelling out math problems to each other. That was how he wanted to spend a lot of his day. Skating and doing math.

The music poured into his ears, but in the distance, Nate thought he heard a voice. He turned around and saw his father waving and calling from the other end of the hallway.

Nate grabbed the earbuds from his ears. *"What?"* he yelled.

"I thought that maybe before Funswamp you and I could go over a few word lists." His father tentatively held out a stack of index cards.

"Dad," said Nate. "I've been playing *all day*. I'm wiped."

"Okay," said Larry. "Say no more." Even from all the way down the hall, Nate could see his disappointment. The sight of this bothered him, and so Nate sighed, then headed back toward the hotel room.

One more day, Nate told himself. *One more day, and then I will be done forever.*

If only it could be that easy.

Chapter Fourteen

WHAT THE GATOR KNEW

As the coach buses pulled up to the amusement park, an irritating song groaned from the loudspeakers strung up over the entrance:

> "FUNSWAMP IS THE FUNNIEST SWAMP
>
> IT'S THE SWAMPIEST FUN IN THE WHOLE
>   WIDE WORLD
>
> HO HO HO AND HA HA HA
>
> COME MEET OUR GATOR
>
> 'CAUSE THERE'S NO GATOR GREATER
>
> THAN AT . . . FUNNNNNNN . . . SWAMP!"

And then the song began all over again.

Duncan pressed his face against the bus window and looked out. The amusement park was lit up with hundreds of brilliant lights. WELCOME YST! read a banner over the archway.

All the players from the YST were given wristbands and ushered out of the buses. "Stay in groups of at least two!" they were told. "Don't get lost!" And, of course, "Have fun!"

If there was anything word-related or educational about Funswamp, it was well hidden. As everyone pushed through the turnstiles into the park, Duncan Dorfman could smell the sweet stink of cotton candy, and the aroma of shining hot dogs as they turned on the rotating rods of their grills.

Funswamp was sort of the opposite of the Scrabble tournament, and yet it filled up another part of him that had long been empty: The amusement park part; the part that craved *junk*.

"Whoa, look at this place," Duncan said to Nate, who stood beside him.

"Yeah, it's totally cheesy," said Nate. He had been to many amusement parks in his life, but this one was probably the worst ever. Nate took in the sight of the cruddy-looking rides, and the adults dressed as reptiles and amphibians walking around having their pictures taken with kids.

"I *wuv* you," said a seven-foot-tall alligator, hugging a child.

"I wuv you, too, Scaly," said the child. "Can I touch your scales?"

"Sure, but be careful, little one, because they're rough!"

The Scrabble kids had until ten P.M., at which point they needed to be back on the buses. Nate's father wandered over to the water-balloon toss, and Nate's mother and Dr. Steve and Eloise headed to the frozen custard stand. "Have a great time, Nate," called Dr. Steve.

Carl Slater's mother sat at the entrance of a kiddie helicopter ride, secretly lighting a cigarette into her cupped hand. Other parents stood in clusters, knowing that they needed to give their kids freedom tonight. Playing in a tournament took a lot out of you. You needed to unwind, or else you might fall apart.

Duncan felt a little concerned when he thought about his mother lying in the hotel room with a migraine, but April yanked him by the arm and insisted he go with her on the gator coaster, and so he forgot about his mother for a while.

April pulled up the safety bar on the first car, locking them in. "Lucy can't handle roller coasters," she said. "She basically turns into a vomit machine. It's her one weakness. Other than that, she's pretty perfect."

"I don't mind going on this ride," Duncan said. "It really doesn't look so bad."

"You *did* see the second hill, right?"

"No," said Duncan. He had only seen the first hill, a gentle rise that wasn't very high. "What do you mean?"

April didn't say anything.

"April, tell me what you mean!" Duncan said again, but it was too late; the roller coaster cars were already rumbling slowly up a gentle hill. He wouldn't be able to get off now. They reached the top, trembled there for a moment, then rushed downward. The wind lifted Duncan's and April's hair; neither of them needed to scream, for the hill was low and the ride was brief.

But then, up ahead, Duncan saw what was coming. The track was almost vertical. It seemed to take forever to reach the top, and when they did, the whole snaking chain of cars paused for an agonizing moment, with Duncan and April right in front.

"Oh my God," Duncan said.

The coaster plunged down so fast that neither of them had a chance to say another word. Their mouths opened into two letter *O*'s, perfectly round and worth one point apiece, and they both screamed *"AAAAAAAAAAAAAHHHHH!"* all the way to the bottom.

After recovering, they went on the Ferris wheel together,

which carried them above the park. "This is unbelievable," Duncan said, looking down.

"Yeah, it's an amazing view," said April.

"No, I mean the whole weekend."

"Oh, I know," said April. "I definitely want to come back next year, no matter what happens tomorrow. Whether we make it to the finals or not." She looked out over the park, her hand shielding her eyes.

"That stuff you were telling everyone," Duncan suddenly said. "I think you'll get what you want. Your family will have to see how good you are. And that the game *is* a sport. At least, it is to you."

"Thanks, Duncan. I think you'll get what you want, too," she said, but he thought she was just being polite.

If the Drilling Falls team didn't win, then everything in Duncan's life would be miserable again. Carl would drop him; it would be as if their friendship, their partnership, had never happened. Duncan and his mother would stay in Aunt Djuna's house for good. He would be Lunch Meat once again, and probably forever.

Tomorrow, during one of the games, when it was no longer possible to win through luck or skill, Duncan would finally have to use the power in the fingertips of his left hand. He wouldn't be able to put it off any longer.

A moment would arise, and he'd go for it, and afterward

he would feel a little ashamed. What had started off as a strange and uncommon skill had become something that made him unhappy. He just wanted to play Scrabble the regular way, like everyone else at the tournament. Was that too much to ask?

Duncan lifted his left hand now and studied it in the nighttime light of the amusement park. It looked like an ordinary hand, like a miniature version of Duncan himself: a little bit chunky and pale.

"I'm not sure I *should* get what I want," he said to April.

"Why not?"

"You have to understand what a weird year this has been," he said, but then he didn't know what else to say. "At first, they called me Lunch Meat."

"Who did?"

"Everybody," he said bitterly.

"But why?"

He told April about the piece of baloney that had been flung onto the back of his ugly yellow shirt.

"What a stupid name," she said. "*Lunch Meat*. It isn't even clever. It's just . . . *nothing*."

"*I* was a nothing," he said. "And then things changed."

"What do you mean?"

He was desperate to tell her all about his power, to confess everything to her and see what she said. But he couldn't tell her, of course, because she might be furious with him. She might even turn him in. She might lose respect for him, too.

"Maybe it's not right to get what I want," he said. "Other people want things, too." He thought of how April had been practicing Scrabble with Lucy for months and months. And then, of course, there were Nate and Maxie to think about. Nate Saviano needed to free himself from his father's death grip. It would devastate Larry Saviano if Nate and Maxie lost, and it would make Nate's life really difficult. "Everything's so *complicated*," Duncan said.

"Everything's always complicated," April said. "Welcome to the world, Duncan."

"We can't *both* win," Duncan said. "One of our teams might win the final round, but of course that would mean the other one loses."

"Or else neither of us might win," said April. "Face it, there are lots of other good teams here. Nate and Maxie could win, easily—look at how Nate plays, and how both of them do that amazing mental math. Or the Surfer Dudes; they're very solid players."

April squinted out over the park. Though she'd insisted that she'd given up on finding the boy from the motel pool—the boy from the past—she was obviously still looking for him. Maybe he was out there in the night. Probably, though, he wasn't.

You never really knew for sure what was going to happen next in life, Duncan thought. That was part of the pain, and the fun. You never knew the end of the story until it happened.

"Maxie, watch this!" Nate Saviano called, chucking a small beanbag toward the center hole at the beanbag-toss booth. But the edge of it caught on the wood and instead of going in it slid down the board.

"Nice try," said Maxie, and she picked up another beanbag and sailed it through the center hole.

A bored teenager with a gigantic Adam's apple handed her a stuffed animal that was meant to look like Scaly the Gator.

"Thanks. It can be our shared pet," said Maxie.

"We can have joint custody," said Nate.

"You can feed it and walk it," Maxie said. "I'll just do the easy stuff, like teach it tricks."

They tossed the alligator back and forth as they walked through the park. It actually did feel a little scaly, Nate thought, yawning. He was tired from the long day, and he wanted to be sure to get a good night's sleep tonight— though probably his father would try and convince him to stay up late studying ING endings or something.

When the evening was almost over, the life-sized Scaly the Gator approached the group of kids, calling through his snout, "Last chance to go on the Lazy Swamp Ride before the park closes!" He managed to herd several players over to the line for the ride.

Nate and Maxie saw their friends heading there, and they joined the cluster and slipped into the very first two-person boat, which waited in a man-made channel of water.

"Here we go, just us and our pet," said Maxie, placing the stuffed animal between them.

Duncan and Carl got into the boat right behind them, trailed by the girls from Portland, and the Surfer Dudes, and then a few other teams. The man in the gator costume called out, "Everyone make sure your seat belt is on!" Then he pulled a lever, and the caravan of boats entered the tunnel. Suddenly it was dark, and the whole place smelled of machine oil. Nate heard the sound of water dripping, and kids giggling and talking in other boats.

Up ahead, a light clicked on in a life-sized diorama, revealing two animatronic alligators in rocking chairs, rocking back and forth. One of them was missing an eye; it had probably rolled off into the water months earlier.

"Pleased to meetcha!" said one of the alligators.

"Be sure to keep your hands out of the water!" said the other. "Our son Junior can get pretty frisky!"

All of a sudden, from within the oily dark water around the boats, another animatronic alligator's head popped up.

Duncan Dorfman peered calmly down at it. Its jaws opened so wide he could see the gears inside. He could even make out a Phillips-head screw that had been screwed into a rod that held the teeth in place.

"This is the lamest ride in the world," Carl muttered beside Duncan.

"Yeah, it really is," Duncan agreed.

From a couple of cars behind them, one of the Surfer Dudes said in his recognizable voice, "Actually, it's totally rad. *Not.*" His partner snickered.

"I've had enough already. We should be in the hotel, resting our brains," said Carl. He turned to Duncan. "You're definitely going to come through tomorrow, right, Duncan?"

But Duncan said nothing.

"*Right*, Duncan? No more *guilty conscience*. It's getting old."

Duncan didn't have time to reply, for they had lurched forward, moving through the dark water toward the next lit-up display. This one was made to look like a scene from Little Red Riding Hood, with an animatronic alligator dressed as a grandmother lying in a bed. A mannequin dressed as Little Red Riding Hood stood beside her.

"Come a little closer, why don'tcha!" said the grandmother.

So Little Red Riding Hood did, and the alligator

reached out with its snapping jaws and grabbed Little Red Riding Hood's head, which neatly popped off. A few kids in the boats appreciatively cried out *"Whoa!"* and *"Nice!"*

"I have to urinate!" cried someone else. Duncan realized it was Tim, from the Wranglers.

"The alligator theme doesn't even make sense," Maxie said to Nate as they sat in their boat. "I mean, what's the point of doing Little Red Riding Hood with *alligators*? What's the point of this whole creepy place?"

"Don't ask me," said Nate.

Without warning, the light in the display—and all the other lights in the tunnel—snapped off, leaving the ride in darkness.

Someone gasped; another kid screamed. Nate and Maxie's boat pushed through the water with a grinding noise. An ominous *KRRRRR* sound came from beneath the surface, and Nate felt himself thrust through some damp rubber flaps, and then he and Maxie Roth were out of the dark tunnel and back in the amusement park, where all the lights were blazing, and the music was playing, and everything was normal.

"That was so odd," Maxie said. "Technical difficulties, I guess."

"I guess," said Nate, a little shaken up. They stood up in their boat and disembarked at the same place where they had gotten on. But when Nate turned around, he saw that none of the other boats had come out of the ride. "Where is everyone?" he asked.

They were the only ones to have made it out of the Lazy Swamp Ride. All the others were still stuck inside.

Chapter Fifteen
TRAPPED

W hat's going on?" Duncan whispered. It was so dark in the tunnel that he couldn't even see Carl, who, in the hurry to get on the ride, had ended up beside him.

"No idea," said Carl Slater, and for once he actually sounded unsure of himself.

"I've been in blackouts before," said a voice with a Southern accent from a few boats back. Duncan recognized it as belonging to Kaylie, one of the Evangelical Scrabblers. "These things happen," Kaylie said.

"Maybe to *you*," said one of the Surfer Dudes. "But not to us. We haven't been in blackouts. We've been in *wipeouts.*"

Their voices all sounded loud and clear, and they could hear one another perfectly.

"I'm sure it will be fixed ASAP," said Lucy Woolery.

"Is ASAP any good in Scrabble?" asked Tim from the Wranglers.

"Of course not," said Carl, snorting.

"Hey, be nice to him, Carl," said April. "He's younger than you."

It was funny, Duncan thought, the way everybody seemed to know exactly who was speaking, even though they were all stuck in a completely dark tunnel. It wasn't the worst place to be trapped. But just as he thought this, he became aware of a *swishing* sound in the water.

"What's *that*?" asked Josh, the other Evangelical Scrabbler.

"Oh, it's probably just the mechanical gears down there," said Lucy. "Nothing to get freaked about."

"Anyway, the live alligators in the park are in enclosed swamp areas," April said. "Lucy and I bought little meat snacks for them from a vending machine. A dollar fifty for a piece of gross, fatty meat. I feel sorry for the alligators here."

"Could be a shark," said one of the Surfer Dudes.

"Cut it out," Duncan said. "You're scaring people."

"By which you mean," said the other Surfer Dude, "we're scaring *you*."

"Yeah, right," said Duncan, but in a way he was a little nervous, and he knew that the Surfer Dudes knew it. Probably everyone did.

They were all silent. Finally Kaylie said, "Maybe this isn't a regular blackout. Nobody's made an announcement to tell us what's happening."

"Do you think someone's going to rescue us?" asked Tim, his voice starting to shake.

"Oh, I'm sure they will," said Lucy. "One of these days."

Time passed, and the little boats rocked slightly in the water, and still no one came to get them out.

"Hello," said Kaylie quietly.

"Hello," said Duncan.

"I wasn't talking to you, Duncan, sorry."

"Oh. Who were you talking to?"

"God."

"Really? Wow," said Lucy Woolery.

"I like to do that when I'm in a stressful situation," Kaylie said.

"And does it help?" Lucy asked.

"Definitely," said Kaylie. "It makes me feel better. You guys can make fun of me if you like. Other kids do."

"People make fun of me, too," said Tim. "Because I look like I'm eight. My dad says I'll probably need human growth hormone injections. You get them every day in your arm or your leg."

"I know a kid who had those," said April. "He said they weren't bad. But anyway, we're not making fun of any of you." She paused. "I get made fun of by my sisters and my brother for liking words so much. They're really annoying about it."

"I get made fun of," said one of the Surfer Dudes, whose name was Jonno, "by my partner, Bradley, when we're surfing and I can't handle a wave."

"That's a total lie," said Bradley.

"No, it's not. You're like, 'What a baby; that wave was like two inches high.'"

"If someone makes fun of us this weekend when Kaylie and I are praying before a game," Josh said, "we're just going to ignore them. We decided this in advance."

"Do you guys think God's here right this minute?" Tim asked. "At Funswamp?"

"Oh, sure," said Kaylie. "Funswamp *needs* God."

"And do you think God is here with us on this ride?" asked Tim.

"I personally happen to think so," Josh said.

There was silence again. No one had any idea how long it would be before they got out of here. They all sat in their boats in the darkness and waited.

Outside, Nate was anxiously trying to get the attention of the guy dressed as Scaly the Gator, who sat on a stool by the lever of the ride. The alligator seemed distracted. "Excuse me, sir," Nate said. "I was on the ride in there, and it got stuck, and then there was a loud grinding sound, and my friend and I got out, but no one else did."

The alligator looked at him. "Is that right?" he said.

"Yes! There are several boats of kids still inside the ride now. They're *trapped* in there," said Nate. "You've got to do something!"

"Well, the park is pretty busy right now," said the alligator. "I can call the manager, but I think he's handling a fried dough emergency."

"A fried dough emergency?" said Nate, and he began to shout. "A FRIED DOUGH EMERGENCY? Are you serious? My friends are stuck inside a pitch-black tunnel filled with water, and it's nighttime, and the park is going to close soon, and we're all playing in a big tournament tomorrow. Everyone needs a good night's sleep! They can't spend the night on the Lazy Swamp Ride!"

"Okay, okay," said the alligator. "I'll see what I can do."

He lumbered off, dragging the heavy load of his tail.

Nate had had enough. "Come on," he said to Maxie. "We can't wait for this guy to get his act together. We have to go back in there and help everyone."

"Nate, we can't do that," said Maxie.

"All right, you stay here and I'll do it."

"I mean, like, we *literally* can't do it," said Maxie. "All the boats are inside. How are we supposed to get back in? Use our skateboards?"

"No," said Nate.

"Go in the water?" said Maxie.

No one else was standing on the platform beside the channel of water. Nate rolled up his pant leg and stuck in a foot. The water felt cool, but not cold.

Nate Saviano was a city kid who had skateboarded through the streets and skate parks of New York, the wind in his face. One afternoon, earlier that year, he had been mugged on the street walking home from the grocery store. Two kids who looked about sixteen had come up to him, and one of them said, "Give us your iPod and all your money." So he'd quickly handed over his new iPod and his wallet, which had exactly three dollars in it, and they had run off laughing while Nate, his heart pounding but somehow his mind staying calm, went up to a newsstand and asked the man inside to call the police.

But he had never waded through a "swamp" in his life. "I've got to do this, Maxie," he said.

"Exactly what are you going to do?"

In answer, Nate lowered himself into the water.

"Whoa," said Maxie Roth. "Be careful, man."

Nate had no idea how deep it would be, and he was relieved when the water level stopped at his thighs. Even with his shoes on, he could feel the slippery bottom. With a shiver, he made his way through the water toward the opening of the tunnel. He pushed through the rubber flaps and found himself back inside the darkness.

When Wendell Bruno, who was still dressed as Scaly the Gator, calmly told Larry Saviano that he had trapped a bunch of kids from the tournament inside the Lazy Swamp Ride, Larry couldn't believe it. "What do you mean, you trapped them inside? Why would you *do* that?"

"I just wanted to tire out the best teams a little," said Wendell. "To keep them at the park longer, and make them a little bit exhausted, so that they wouldn't concentrate as well in the morning. Nate wasn't supposed to be among them, but he got on the ride before I noticed. Luckily he was in the first car, so I managed to get him out."

The two men stood by the caramel corn booth, the smell overpowering them. A little while earlier, Larry had realized that he couldn't find his son; in fact, he couldn't find any of the kids Nate had been hanging around with at the tournament. They all seemed to have disappeared in one clump, like the astronauts who had been whisked back in time in Larry's *Zax* novels.

"Have you become a *maniac* over the past twenty-six years?" asked Larry.

"I told you that I had a plan," said Wendell Bruno. "You said you were glad."

"A plan to trap a group of kids inside a ride in order to tire them out for the games tomorrow?"

"It wasn't meant to be *all* of them, Larry. What am I, stupid? The whole point was that Nate and Maxie would be the ones to have a relaxed evening tonight, while all the other strong players would be a little . . . tuckered out. It was a totally harmless prank. Lighten up."

"I cannot believe you would do this," said Larry. "To minors!"

"Oh, that's a good one," said Wendell, shaking his large alligator head. "I believe *you're* the one who makes your boy study Scrabble words day and night, am I right?"

"That's an exaggeration."

"Look," said Wendell, "we both know that losing the tournament made us each a little crazy. As I was about to tell you, my plan to jam the ride and tucker out the kids didn't work out exactly the way it was supposed to. Who knew you would have such a goody-goody son? The long hair and the skateboard and the hipster, ultra-pierced skater-girl partner sure fooled me."

"What are you talking about?"

"Nate went back inside to get his friends out," said Wendell. "The woman who's dressed as Cuddly the Iguana told me she saw a long-haired kid slip inside. Cuddly knows everything that goes on at Funswamp."

"What? Nate's inside?"

"Yes. He waded into the water."

"Isn't that dangerous?" said Larry.

"Nah. The only thing that could go wrong is there could be a sudden electrical current in the water. But the chances of that happening are as low as . . . the chances of getting a bingo-bango-bongo."

"An *electrical current*?" Larry was terrified and angry, but he had to take action. "Go get a flashlight from a security guard, Wendell. We're going in."

Wendell found a flashlight, and he and Larry jogged through the crowd toward the Lazy Swamp Ride. Together, the man and the alligator stepped into the water.

But inside the ride, Duncan was wondering something. This fingertip ability of his, this "power"—was it good for anything real?

Was it actually *useful*, or was it just some kind of cheater's trick?

Quietly, without calling attention to himself, Duncan reached his left hand out and ran it along the slimy wall in the darkness.

Carl sensed movement and understood what Duncan was doing. "Getting anything?" Carl whispered. "Picking up any information?"

"Not yet," said Duncan. For a foot or so there was just

a stretch of algae-covered wall, and then, finally, there was a sign. Duncan ran his hand across it, waiting, waiting. Within seconds his fingertips began to heat up. They were like five hot little pokers, and together they worked to lift the letters on the sign to life. "Emergency Equipment," he read aloud.

"Fantastic," said Carl.

"Break glass below," Duncan kept reading. "Anybody got anything heavy?" he called out.

"I have my Scrabble dictionary," Josh admitted. "The hardcover edition."

Somehow the dictionary was handed over in the darkness from boat to boat, and Duncan rammed it against the panel of glass he had now located with his hand. All he heard was a dull thud. Some of the kids said "Ohhh," and "Too bad," so he tried again. Nothing.

"Oh, for once in your life don't be such a weakling, Dorfman," Carl said, starting to grab the book from him, but Duncan didn't want to give it over. This time he slammed the dictionary against the glass panel, and it broke with a resounding shatter that sounded like falling icicles.

Duncan carefully reached inside and felt around. His fingers gripped the edges of a big flashlight, and he took it out and switched it on. The whole area was illuminated, and he could see the players' faces, some frightened, some relieved, some (the Surfer Dudes') smirking. He also reached back in through the panel and pulled out a couple of emergency oars, and handed them over to the others. Slowly, Lucy and April were able to push off and start to paddle.

"All right, how did you *do* that?" asked the Surfer Dude Jonno, looking directly at Duncan.

"Do what?" said Duncan innocently.

"Read the words on the wall." Jonno gestured toward the sign that read EMERGENCY EQUIPMENT. "You read it out loud in the darkness. I *heard* you."

"Yeah, we all heard you," echoed his partner, Bradley. The two of them were big and blond and menacing with their sharks' teeth hanging on leather straps around their ample necks.

But Duncan didn't have to answer, for distantly there came splashing, and the sound of voices. A flashlight beam appeared in the long tunnel, and Nate Saviano was standing in the water. "There you are!" Nate called.

Coming up behind him, his father sloshed through the water as swiftly as he could. Beside him, Wendell Bruno pushed through with more effort, his furry, clanking wet costume slowing him down.

When Tim from the Wranglers team saw the alligator in the water, he began to fall apart. "It's an alligator!" he cried. And then he added, "I have to urinate!"

"Come on, Tim, do you *really* have to urinate?" Duncan gently asked him.

"Yes! Yes, I do!" said Tim. After a moment he added, with wonder, "No, actually, I don't. I just *thought* I did."

"You're fine," said Duncan. "Just take it easy, okay?"

"But there's still an alligator coming toward us," said Tim.

"You're frightening that kid," Larry Saviano hissed to Wendell. "He thinks you're an actual alligator."

"Tim, use your head," said Duncan. "That is just a grown man dressed as Scaly the Gator. Listen, Tim," he went on, "can you figure out a five-letter anagram for SCALY?"

Tim blew his nose. "Is it an obscure word?"

"No," said Duncan. "Not the one I'm thinking of."

"CLAYS," said Tim after a beat.

"Nice work," said Duncan.

"And ACYLS is good, too," Lucy couldn't help but add.

Nate's father and Wendell Bruno helped Nate push the boats back out though the tunnel. Nate was completely confused. Why was his dad here? And how did he know this guy dressed in the alligator costume, anyway? What was going on?

Just as the Scrabble players emerged, climbing back up onto the dock, a bright flash came from inside the tunnel, and they heard a loud electrical snap. A shower of sparks poured through the flaps.

"What was *that*?" someone asked. Later, they all found out that there had been an electrical short in the covered wires snaking beneath the water.

But as it was, no one had been hurt or even tired out by getting stuck in the ride. And it didn't, in the end, affect the outcome of the tournament.

But it was *strange*, Nate thought as he sat wrapped in a towel on the bus heading back to the hotel, that his father had been in the tunnel with that man in the alligator costume. That man who, when he finally took off his alligator head, was revealed to be the bald guy who had been seen staring at Nate earlier in the day. The dark glasses were off now, but April and Lucy had immediately recognized him and let Nate know.

Something peculiar was going on, but Nate Saviano couldn't figure it out.

A little later, back in the hotel room, his father ran him a vanilla-citrus-scented bubble bath. "Take your time," Larry Saviano said. "I'll order us some hot soup from room service. And be sure to give your mom and stepdad a call in their room down the hall. They were so worried about you when you came off the ride all wet. Dr. Steve practically wanted to put you in an iron lung."

"An iron what? I wasn't going to get sick from being wet. We're in Florida, Dad, not Alaska," Nate reminded him. "I'll be fine. But yeah, I'll give them a call."

Father and son stood in the big marble bathroom. Larry turned off the taps and said, "Your bath awaits," then walked out of the room to give him privacy.

"Dad?" Nate said. His father turned around. "Who was that guy?" Nate asked.

His father paused. "Which guy?"

"You *know* which guy!" said Nate, his loud voice echoing off all the marble. He didn't want to use his "inside voice" now. "Come on, Dad," he said. "Don't act like you don't know what I'm talking about."

His father sighed and shook his head. "All right," he said. "Nate, listen, I've got to tell you something. You might want to skip the bath for now, kid."

Nate drained the water from the tub and followed his father back into the hotel room, where they sat facing each other on the beds. Mints in silver foil had been placed on the pillows earlier, but they just left them there. "Go ahead," Nate said.

His father said, "The man in the alligator suit is Wendell Bruno."

Nate heard himself gasp. "Your Scrabble partner?"

"Yes. He lives right here in Yakamee," his father continued. "It's the first time I've seen him in twenty-six years."

Larry told Nate about how Wendell Bruno had deliberately jammed the Lazy Swamp Ride in order to tire everyone else out a little. "In his defense, I should say that he's not a criminal," Larry said. "Just a weak person. He still can't get over losing."

"And neither can you," Nate said.

"That's true. Losing the tournament changed the path of both our lives."

"And my life, too, in case you hadn't noticed," said Nate.

"Yes, your life, too," said Larry. "And I'm sorry about that, Nate, I really am. I know I'm tough with you. But I'm hoping that after the weekend's over, I'll be able to move on. And now," he added, "there are *two* of us counting on you, not just one."

Nate looked at his father. He imagined him as a twelve-year-old sitting on a bed in this very hotel, twenty-six years earlier. Of course, Larry wouldn't have had a beard then. In some ways, though, Nate's father was the same person now that he'd always been. Larry and Wendell had just been two boys who played Scrabble a lot and wanted to do well.

Nate felt sorry for his father for being so unrelentingly competitive. There were a few kids at the YST who were like that; Carl Slater was one of them, Nate knew, and so, he'd heard, were the Surfer Dudes. But most of the kids here weren't that way at all.

"Dad, it's an amazing story, but I've got to get some sleep," Nate said finally. "I've got a big day tomorrow. A huge day."

For once, his father didn't try and stop him. In silence they crunched on the mints from their pillows, and then Nate got into bed.

The Blunt family let themselves into their hotel suite after the long night at Funswamp. Jenna turned on *Thwap!* TV, which was broadcasting a basketball game. Everyone sat around and watched it, and after a moment, because she had nothing else to do, April joined them. To her surprise, the game was very exciting.

She noticed, for the first time, that the players kept their eyes on the ball the same way she kept her eyes on the tiles. "Shoot!" she found herself calling out when a player paused and dribbled before the basket. "Shoot!" Her whole family turned to her, shocked.

"April?" said her brother, Gregory. "Was that *you*?"

"Yes," she said. She was as surprised by her outcry as they were. April imagined herself on that screen, being televised as she played the final round of the YST. She pictured her family watching her as if she were a basketball player in the crucial last seconds of a game. Everyone in her family would be rooting harder for the Oregonzos than they had ever rooted for any other team.

Up on the eighteenth floor, Duncan Dorfman's mother was sitting up in bed with the light on, reading a book.

"Oh good," Duncan said as he entered the room. "You're feeling better, Mom?"

"Much. Stupid migraine finally went away," she said, closing her book. "I was really sorry to miss the amusement park. Was it fun?"

Duncan plunked himself down on the other bed and said, "Only if your idea of fun is being trapped inside a ride, and then being rescued by another player's father and an alligator."

"*Excuse* me?"

Duncan explained what had happened. "It was really strange, sitting in the dark for so long," he said. "Not knowing when we'd get out. But I think maybe I helped a little."

"That's good; I'm glad to hear it. What a night," his mother said. "And you had quite a day too. By the way, I took a look at the pair of pants you changed out of, Duncan. That rip in the knee, and all that blood! You must have *really* hurt yourself. It wasn't an ordinary fall that you took, was it?"

Duncan paused, remembering how hard he had landed when he flew off the skateboard. "No," he said. "Not exactly."

"Don't tell me," his mother said, raising her hand up. "I don't want to know. I know I'm overprotective. I know I need to give you a little more independence. You've had a hard year, moving to a new state, giving up our home. And even if things don't go your way tomorrow, I hope you'll be okay with it. You're a terrific person, and that's what matters."

But Duncan had to wonder if he was all that terrific. A terrific person probably wouldn't have lied his way here. A terrific person wouldn't do what Duncan Dorfman knew he was finally going to have to do tomorrow when reaching into the tile bag. As far as he could see, there was no other way.

Chapter Sixteen
THE END IS NEAR

And yet, by the last moments of round four the next morning, Duncan still couldn't bring himself to use his fingertips.

Four minutes and eighteen seconds were left on Drilling Falls' timer, and he and Carl were losing badly. The score was 225 to 301, and their opponents, the Surfer Dudes, were on a roll. The team from Malibu had recently made a high-scoring bingo; then they'd played ZA with the Z landing on a double-letter square in two directions. Both times, they'd high-fived each other with their clamshell-sized hands. Their Hawaiian shirts were insanely bright and distracting across the table, and Duncan practically heard the ocean roar in his ears. The situation looked dire.

Do it, he told himself. He reached into the bag with his left hand and let the tiles sift between his fingers. They felt as cool and smooth as sea glass. Carl was now watching him to see what he would do. In that moment, Duncan knew he absolutely had to close his eyes and finally let his mind take him to the place where his brain sent a signal to his fingertips, making them grow hot. Making them sensitive to every bit of ink spattered upon the plastic surface of a factory-made tile.

Do it. But he just couldn't. He still wasn't ready to tilt the game in his favor. He still wasn't ready to almost-cheat. Maybe by the next game he'd be ready, but not yet, not now.

And he also wasn't ready to tell Carl he wasn't ready. Inside the bag, Duncan's fingertips tapped against the tiles. While Carl was watching, Duncan closed his eyes and made it look as if he was concentrating. He wanted to let Carl believe that his fingertips were once again alive with heat.

"Hot," he mouthed to Carl, who smiled, pleased. From across the table, the Surfer Dudes watched with curiosity. Duncan plucked up five tiles and held them in his fist. "Whew," he said to Carl quietly, faking it.

"Let's see what you brought us," whispered Carl. "Let's see your catch."

How bad could the tiles be? Duncan thought. No

matter which ones he had picked, he could try to explain them to Carl later. *You see, I thought selecting the W and the H seemed like a good idea,* he'd say. *I had a strategy in mind . . .*

"Hey, no coffeehousing," said Bradley.

Carl happily pried open the fingers of Duncan's left hand and pulled out the letters. He placed them on the rack so they could both look at them.

They were unbelievable.

Unbelievably bad.

There was *no way* that Carl could think that Duncan had picked these on purpose. He had drawn:

UUUVV

Added to the two I's that were already on their rack, the Drilling Falls team now had one of the worst racks possible in Scrabble.

UUUVVII

You could move those letters around forever and ever, and nothing good would come of them. Carl turned to Duncan with a dropped-open mouth. "What happened?" he said out loud, not even bothering to keep his voice down. "You *did* the thing. The fingertip thing. I saw you do it!"

"I can explain," said Duncan, though he really couldn't. The other Surfer Dude put his finger to his lips and made a warning face. There would be no more coffee-housing, or *else.*

Duncan returned to his tiles, hunching over them and refusing to meet Carl's gaze. Carl angrily wrote on the pad of paper:

LOOK AT ME, DORFMAN!!!!!

But Duncan wouldn't look. The rest of the game was spent in dreadful silence.

In the end, though, through a sudden, last-minute run of luck more than anything else (Carl picked the Q, and played it on QINTAR for 50 points), Drilling Falls beat the Surfer Dudes by four points.

But the Surfer Dudes would not go quietly. Jonno, the slightly bigger and more hulking of the two teammates, stood and loomed over the board. "Something's fishy around here," he said.

"No it isn't," said Carl.

"You did that thing in the darkness on the Lazy Swamp Ride," Jonno said, pointing to Duncan. "You read those words on the wall, when no one could possibly have read them."

"I have twenty-twenty vision," Duncan said faintly. "I took an eye test recently."

"It isn't that," said Bradley, the Surfer Dude with the hair that was slightly more greenish-gold. He leaned farther across the board, his face right in Duncan's face. Duncan could smell his breath; it smelled of the sea, but not in a good way. "You did something with your *hand*," said Bradley.

"Your left hand. And I bet you've been cheating this whole time at the tournament."

"That is not true!" shouted Duncan. Everyone turned and stared at him. There was a whole chorus of *shhh's*, so strong it sounded like the leaves of two hundred trees rustling in a forest.

The Surfer Dudes refused to shake hands with Drilling Falls. Instead, they stormed off, heading to the front of the room. Duncan watched from afar as the Surfer Dudes spoke to the tournament director Dave Hopper, using wild gestures. They pointed toward Duncan, and then, to demonstrate, Jonno reached out his hand toward an imaginary wall, feeling it as if he could read letters on it. Dave Hopper appeared puzzled by the pantomime, and within seconds he ended the conversation with the Surfer Dudes. The boys looked furious.

But the Surfer Dudes weren't the only ones furious with Duncan Dorfman. On his way out of the ballroom, Duncan felt a hard shove against his back that made him stagger forward. He turned around to face Carl, who grabbed him by the front of his Drilling Falls Scrabble Team T-shirt.

"Just what do you think you're doing?" Carl said.

"What do you mean?"

"I know you didn't really use your fingertips."

"The Surfer Dudes think I did. But look, we won anyway," Duncan tried.

"We *barely* won, Dorfman," said Carl, coming so close that Duncan could see the individual pores of Carl's face. "We could have *easily* lost that game. And then we would have had almost no chance of making it to the finals. I brought you all the way down here to *win*, and now look at you! I ought to punch your lights out. I ought to rearrange your nose and your eyeballs, make you look like a *Picasso* painting—"

"Whoa, whoa," said Nate Saviano, who'd strode over. He was holding up his skateboard like a shield, or a weapon. "What's going on?"

"My partner needs some straightening out," Carl muttered.

"I don't think Duncan needs anything at all," said Nate, and Carl backed down, then slunk off. Nate turned to Duncan and said, "You lost? Is that why he's so steamed?"

"No," said Duncan. "We won."

"Huh. Go figure," said Nate.

Duncan took a few seconds to calm down, and then the boys walked out of the ballroom together. "How did you and Maxie do, by the way?" Duncan asked.

"We won, too. So I guess we're all still in this thing."

"You don't look happy about it."

"I'm not," Nate admitted. "I just want out."

Players had begun to flood out of the ballroom, their games over. Everything was starting to sort itself out now, and the teams that had won all of their games knew they had a serious chance to go to the finals. A few kids were talking about how the Word Gurrrls from Minnesota—giggling Jessica and Tania, with the cat's-eye eyeglasses—remained undefeated.

Almost everyone else knew that no matter what happened in the fifth and sixth games, they weren't going to go all the way. But it didn't matter. Most of them were having an excellent time. Some were still curious to see where they would rank. Some couldn't care less about the rankings or standings. Almost all of the players were looking forward to the grand finale of the weekend: watching the final round on a huge screen, with live commentary by sports announcer Bill Preston of *Thwap!* TV.

Round five would begin right after lunch, followed by round six, the critical round—the semifinals, really, though it wasn't officially called that. Now everyone in the group of friends except Carl was sitting together again at a table outside on the patio.

"What's with you and your partner?" Lucy asked Duncan. "It looked like you two were having a fight in there." Duncan told her he didn't want to talk about it.

All of them were quiet as they ate, sinking into seriousness and contemplating their fates. The Oregonzos, the Drilling Falls team, and the Big Apple Duo remained undefeated. The Evangelical Scrabblers were down by one, and still had a remote shot at actually winning the whole event. If Josh and Kaylie were to win games five and six by good spreads, and if they happened to beat an undefeated team in the semifinals, they could go to the finals and win. Unlikely, but not impossible.

The outcome of the tournament was almost too overwhelming for any of them to think about, so instead they all just ate their sandwiches and looked out at the ocean.

"Gorgeous day," said Lucy.

"Yeah, great weather," said Maxie. "I hear it's snowing in New York. Glad I'm not there. Bad skateboard weather."

None of them cared about the weather right now, but they jabbered about it until there was nothing left to say. Then they fell into an excruciating silence.

The gong sounded at shortly before 2:00 P.M., and all the kids returned to the ballroom. This time, not all of them ran inside; some took their time. Duncan moved as slowly as possible, dragging his leg with the bad knee. Though the tension was high, and the possibility that his team might win excited him, he was in no hurry to be back in the ballroom sitting beside Carl, who had begun to hate his guts.

The fifth game, played against Timed Fury, a team of two tall, quiet boys from New Jersey, went by quickly. It was as if someone else was playing the game, and Duncan was watching from a distance. Carl turned and stared as Duncan reached his hand in and out of the bag mechanically.

How could he explain to Carl why he did what he did during the last game? Why he hadn't used his fingertips when he really ought to have? Carl would never understand. Carl seemed to have no moral dilemmas or ambivalence or regret about *anything*. He wanted what he wanted, and usually he got it, too.

Maybe, Duncan thought unhappily, it wasn't the worst thing in the world to be someone like Carl Slater. At least you could enjoy your life.

Duncan and Carl won game five cleanly, swiftly and without tricks, 382–290. There had been a couple of unexciting bingos on both sides. Each team had picked two S's, and the power tiles had been pretty evenly distributed, too. But Drilling Falls had simply thought through their moves more carefully, and so they had won in the end.

As the boys shook hands across the board, Duncan felt mostly numb. He and Carl would be among the teams who still had a chance to go all the way. But this fact alone wasn't enough to make Carl behave any less hostilely toward him. In fact, it only seemed to infuriate Carl even more.

During the break between games five and six, the kids wandered the atrium, and though some of them were so excited they could barely keep it in, Duncan barely felt like speaking. Soon the list was up, and everyone learned who the other top contenders were, and what the pairings would be in the sixth game.

Drilling Falls was going to play the Big Apple Duo, and the Oregonzos would play the Word Gurrrls.

The final moments before round six might have given Duncan a chance to think about what a great job he and Carl had done so far, and how it would feel to play this important game against his friends Nate and Maxie. But instead he simply felt sick with worry. He should never have agreed to come here. Carl should have come with Brian Kalb again, and Duncan should have stayed home at his great-aunt's house. But it was much too late to do anything about it now.

When round six was about to begin, Carl walked over to the table in the ballroom with absolutely no expression on his face. He sat down next to Duncan and busied himself lining up fresh pencils beside the score sheet.

"So you're giving me the silent treatment?" asked Duncan. Carl didn't even look at him. "Yep, I guess there's my answer," Duncan said. "Well, at least we're in no danger of being yelled at for coffeehousing." Carl still said nothing.

"Oh, that's really mature, Carl," said Nate, who had taken his place with Maxie across the board.

Carl Slater looked up and said, "You have no idea what you're dealing with here, Nate, so maybe you should stay out of it." He paused. "Anyway, what do you know? You're just some grungy *skateboarder*. That's all you both are, you and Maxie."

"And you're just some bully," said Maxie. "We have those in New York, too. You guys are everywhere. It's an epidemic. We're going to need a *vaccine*."

Carl folded his arms and leaned across the board. "Nate; Maxie. Look. I was just spouting off. I've got no problem with you two. But Duncan made a promise to me, and he knows it."

Nate looked directly at Carl. "No, you're right about me, Carl," he said.

"What?"

Nate pushed back in his chair and stood up. "I *am* just some grungy skateboarder," he said. "That's what I want to be. I never wanted *this*. And you know what? I am through," he said. He handed the pencil and pad to Maxie. "You're on your own."

Other kids began to notice what was happening at one of the semifinal tables; there was whispering around the room.

"What are you doing, Nate?" Maxie asked.

Over the loudspeaker, Dave Hopper announced, "You may begin."

Maxie frantically reached into the bag and pulled out a tile. "Look, Nate, we got a B," she said. "It's a good start!"

Immediately, Carl reached in and drew an S. The Big Apple Duo would go first in this game.

Maxie reached back into the bag and drew all the tiles for their team. Carl slammed his hand down on the timer, and they all watched as seconds began to fall away from Nate and Maxie's side. But Nate didn't seem to care. He was still standing there, ignoring the clock, ignoring the tiles, and he didn't appear to be kidding around.

"I'm sorry, Maxie," he said. "I just can't do it anymore. I shouldn't have dragged you down here."

"You didn't drag me. I wanted to come. I like you, Nate," she blurted out. "I liked hanging out last year. When you left school, I was really bummed."

"Me too," he said. "This year has been horrible. I didn't want to be in this tournament. So I'm sending a message to my dad right now." He glanced around the room. "Even though I don't see him at the moment," he added.

"What message?"

"Basically: 'Too bad, sucker, you lost again!'" Then, more softly, Nate said, "See you, Maxie," and he picked up his skateboard and left.

The three remaining kids sat at the table, shocked. Other kids looked over, surprised and confused, but then quickly returned to their own games.

"What am I going to do?" said Maxie Roth to Duncan and Carl. "I'm not a real Scrabble player. I'm just a grungy skateboarder, too, like Carl said. I can't play this game alone." Before they could reply, Maxie stood up and grabbed her own skateboard. "See you guys," she said. "It's been real."

Duncan watched the back of her magenta head go away, and the tip of her pink skateboard. Everything about her was unusual and different. And everything about *me*, he thought, is hopeless. Beside him, Carl Slater was staring at Duncan in fury through tiny eye slits.

"So what do we do now?" Duncan asked.

"What do you think we do, Dorfman? We turn cartwheels across the table. We churn our own butter. No, we *sit here*, and we wait for their clock to run down, and for them to forfeit the game because of time. And then we win. Which is the only way that would be certain to happen," he added in disgust, "with *you* as a partner."

"But shouldn't we say something to someone? I mean, I don't know what the rules are if your opponent walks away."

"Don't you dare get up or say a word," said Carl. "Do what you've been doing your whole life, Dorfman: *Just. Do. Nothing.*"

Outside, in the heat of the day, Nate Saviano got on his skateboard. After a moment he heard shouting in the distance, and he turned to see someone coming toward him.

It was Maxie, who cruised up to him on her board. Nate had a feeling she was going to start sobbing and begging him to come back inside the ballroom. They got off their boards and faced each other.

But what she said to him was, "OF ALL THE SELFISH THINGS IN THE WORLD TO DO!"

Nate was startled, because he was usually the one who shouted at other people—at least, he shouted at his father. He was not used to anyone shouting at him. "Selfish?" he said. "How was that selfish?"

"Because we're a team," she said. "You act like it's just you. But, like, HELLO? I'm here, too, Nate. I am your TEAMMATE. This isn't just about you; it also happens to be about me. Do you know that my mom and dad had to scramble to get the money so we could come down here? And I made all my friends at school practice Scrabble with me every day in the month before I came. I put down the skateboard and picked up a *Scrabble* board. I never got good enough to play at this high level on my own, but that's the thing: I knew I was on a TEAM. So fine, if you want to quit the tournament, I can't stop you. I care about how I play. I care about this tournament, okay, Nate? I know I'm not great at the making-words part—I don't know every single one of my twos yet, I don't know how to make a decent bingo—but I'm quick at the math part. And I was really into this whole thing, and now you've ruined it! You know what? I wish you'd never come back to the skate park this fall."

"Whoa, whoa," said Nate, holding up his hands. "I am *not* selfish, Maxie. And I had no idea you cared so much about this tournament."

"Oh, you thought I was just doing it for you, Nate? Well, think again."

Her face was pink with heat; her whole self was pinkish: her face, her hair, her board. He could see how intense she was. He thought about how he'd liked hanging out with her and figuring out the math part of their games—how many points they'd need to win, or tie. She was faster than he was at numbers. It wasn't even true that Nate hated Scrabble—he just hated the pressure to win first place. It hadn't occurred to him that Maxie wanted them to play as well as they could. He hadn't known that the games meant something to her.

Nate knew that he would go back inside now, and he would play this game as hard as he could. He would play it for himself and his partner, Maxie Roth, skatefreak and math whiz, and, it seemed, good friend.

"Come on," Nate said. "We've already lost so much time."

Inside the ballroom, everyone was playing with intense concentration, except for the Drilling Falls team, who sat silently. Duncan had done nothing, exactly the way Carl wanted him to. He hated himself for it, but he knew he wasn't alone in this feeling: Carl hated him, too. Nate and Maxie, who had left the ballroom, had only eight minutes left on their clock.

"You are one lucky dude," Carl whispered to Duncan under his breath. "We're going to win this game by default, Dorfman," he said. "You've escaped my total wrath for now, but just wait until the next round. Then you'd better do what you're supposed to. You'd better use those fingers of yours, the way we agreed."

There was a commotion in the doorway, and Duncan saw the Big Apple Duo tearing into the room with their skateboards under their arms. They were like superheroes come to save the day, but no one knew exactly who they were supposed to save—except perhaps themselves. A couple of kids clapped. The duo landed at table two, slamming their bodies hard into their seats, and then immediately glanced at the clock.

"Okay," said Nate, panting. "We're way low on time, Maxie. Let's get cracking."

Together they began to play.

Carl looked as if he wanted to faint, or kill Duncan. Drilling Falls had been on the verge of the easiest win ever, and now it was ruined. "What?" said Carl. "You're *playing*? You guys don't have time. Just forfeit the game. You have no other choice."

Maxie Roth laughed lightly. "Oh, right," she said. "Sorry, Carl. We didn't come down to Yakamee to throw it all away."

Back and forth the two teams went, picking letters and laying them down. Nate and Maxie worked as quickly as they could, Nate taking the lead on all the strange little Scrabble words, and Maxie figuring out the value of moves in her head. Their speed was impressive, and both teams traded leads. There was a symmetry to the game that made Duncan feel as if it could go on like this forever, which wouldn't have been the worst thing in the world.

But the tile bag was getting rapidly lighter. Carl's expression signaled to Duncan that he needed to do something, and *fast*. Duncan didn't respond. He just reached into the bag and grabbed five tiles. Please, he thought, let them be good ones. Let them be so good that Carl thinks I picked each one on purpose.

He opened his hand and looked, and he was flooded with relief. Duncan had drawn:

S

S

N

A

P

Along with the O and the I that were already on

their rack, it seemed likely that there was a bingo lurking. Together the letters looked like:

ISNAPOS

Carl gave him a pleased look, and a little nod. Duncan nodded back. Together they hunched over the rack. Carl chewed his lip and moved the letters around.

SIONASP

No.

ONSASPI

No.

Suddenly Duncan saw it. There it was, laughably right in front of him—a word he'd heard throughout his life, and which had always had great importance to him.

It was the name of the disease that his father had died of before Duncan was born:

PANOSIS

He knew that if he played this word, he and Carl would take a strong lead. Duncan thought about Nate's father, and how desperate he was for Nate to win and go to the finals. But just because Duncan felt sorry for Nate, he knew he shouldn't let the Big Apple Duo win. It wouldn't have been any more honest than using his fingertips.

Without checking with Carl first, Duncan picked up all the letters on his rack and laid them down on the board. He was sure of this bingo. So sure that he even hit the clock right away, just as Carl had done yesterday, to Duncan's irritation. Carl looked irritated now, too, but then he was pleased. PANOSIS was worth 78 points, after all.

"Challenge," Nate Saviano said.

"What?" said Duncan, looking up.

"Challenge," Nate repeated.

Carl seemed a little nervous about this, but Duncan stayed calm. He was positive that this word was good. After all, it was one of the most significant words of his entire life. Nate and Maxie would lose the challenge, Duncan knew. He and Nate and Carl and Maxie now stood up from the table and walked toward one of the word-judge machines.

PANOSIS, Duncan typed, and Nate pressed ENTER.

A new screen popped up, its border bright red, its message seeming to scream at Duncan Dorfman, mocking him and everything he had ever known:

NO, THIS PLAY IS NO GOOD

"That's wrong," said Duncan. "It is too a word."

"Sorry, Duncan," Nate said softly. "The computer says it isn't."

Duncan looked at Nate, who showed no triumph; Nate even seemed concerned that Duncan was upset.

"PANOSIS is no good?" Carl asked, astonished. "But you acted like you *knew* it was good, Dorfman. You were so completely sure of yourself. And you're *never* sure of yourself!"

They all returned to the table. "It *is* good, Carl," Duncan insisted in a whisper. "I just don't understand. Maybe . . . it's like SPORK. Everyone knows it's a real *thing*, but the people who make the rules say it isn't."

"No coffeehousing!" a girl warned from the next table, and Duncan and Carl went silent.

Nate pried the tiles up from the board, and now Nate and Maxie were given a free turn. They played MAYO for 26 points, putting them in the lead. Duncan churned in his chair, not understanding what had happened. It was crazy that the computer hadn't accepted PANOSIS! Of course it was a real word. Panosis was a rare but fatal disease, and it had taken Duncan's father away from him and his mother over twelve years earlier. But you weren't allowed to argue with the computer during a tournament; it had the final word on all challenges.

Just when Duncan thought that there wouldn't be a way to use his fingertips to save the game at this late stage even if he *wanted* to, Carl smiled slyly.

"*Watch this,*" Carl mouthed, and then he picked up the letters in PANOSIS from the rack and placed them on the board, hooking off the O in MAYO in a different order. They now spelled:

PASSION

"*Whoa,*" said Duncan, and the tension between them broke for now.

At the end of the game, Duncan and Carl surged ahead

to beat the team from New York City by 56 points. Even after the Big Apple Duo's late comeback—their dramatic return to the ballroom, and the way they had managed their tiles with no time to spare—they still hadn't been able to pull it out. Nate and Maxie weren't going to the finals.

But Duncan and Carl were. Duncan had helped his team come this far without once using the power in his fingertips. He lingered at the board for an extra moment now, thinking anxiously about how, during the final round against either the giggling, feverish World Gurrrls or the Oregonzos, the tension with Carl would definitely return, cranked up as high as it could humanly go.

Duncan had sworn to Carl that he would use his fingertips when he absolutely had to. If the finals of the Youth Scrabble Tournament didn't count as an "absolutely have to" situation, then what did? But Duncan couldn't cope with that thought yet.

Right now, he stood to shake hands with Nate and Maxie across the table, and in the background there was a buzz of interest, because everyone saw that there had been an outcome at one of the semifinalists' tables. The first team of finalists had been chosen. Maxie looked fierce, as she always did, and proud. After the New York team congratulated Drilling Falls, Maxie said to Nate, "I can't believe we made it this far. I mean, like, it's pretty amazing, isn't it?"

But Nate, who had almost quit the tournament,

looked surprisingly upset. "My dad is going to flip out," he said. "He's just not going to be able to stand it. He's going to make me start preparing for next year's tournament, and my life will remain a living hell."

"You want me to come tell him with you?" Duncan asked.

Nate shook his head. "Nah, thanks anyway."

"I could come," said Maxie. "I'm your partner."

"Thanks, you guys," said Nate. "But I think I should do this alone."

Nate Saviano tucked his skateboard under his arm and walked out of the ballroom. His father was somewhere out there, and Nate would have to find him and tell him it was over.

On the other side of the ballroom, the game between the Evangelical Scrabblers and a team from Maryland was reaching its climax. The two teams had played seriously and tensely, but in the end Maryland won. Hands were shaken. Kaylie and Josh both looked a little shocked at their loss, but they still forced themselves to say "Good job," and "Congratulations."

Then the Evangelical Scrabblers stood and held hands, looking upward and becoming very still.

"We didn't embarrass ourselves at all this weekend," Kaylie whispered. "We won some games, and we played hard. And we really had an awesome time."

"Plus, I'd like to add that we got room service late last night," whispered Josh. "And that was really cool. I had chicken fingers with honey-mustard dipping sauce. But I guess you already know that."

"Thank you," Kaylie said firmly, and Josh echoed, "Thank you," too. Then they ran off to see their family.

The atrium was now crowded with players being hugged by mothers, fathers, siblings, and coaches. When Duncan saw his own mother, she approached him cautiously, uncertain of how to read the expression on his face.

"Duncan, I'm not sure if this is good or bad," she said, coming closer.

He waited until she was right in front of him, and then he smiled and said, "We did it, Mom. We made it to the finals!"

His mother let out a scream, then she threw her arms around him. "Oh, Duncan, that's wonderful!" she cried. "I have to go call Aunt Djuna! And just think, when we first moved to Drilling Falls, you couldn't play Scrabble at all!"

Duncan and his mother hugged for a few seconds. After they were done, and had both agreed how exciting this was, and had talked about how there was only *one hour* until the final round was to begin, he mentioned the detail from the last game that still bothered him. "Here's something weird: Carl and I," he said, "lost a challenge on a word that was obviously good."

"What was it?" she asked.

"PANOSIS."

Duncan's mother's expression immediately changed. She'd been so happy, but now she looked stiff and upset. "That's odd," she said.

"I know," said Duncan. "I think the word-judge program should update its dictionary. I mean, apparently they added ZA a bunch of years ago, and QI, and a few others. It's time they added PANOSIS. And while they're at it, SPORK. Yes, I will definitely write them a letter about SPORK."

"Duncan!" April called, running over along with Lucy, both of them flushed and excited. "We've been looking for you!"

"We heard you guys won," said Lucy, breathless. "Everyone's talking about it. Well, guess what? We just beat the Word Gurrrls. Jessica and Tania. They giggled throughout the game, though maybe it was just a strategy to throw us off, but I doubt it. I think they just had the giggles. But the point is, it's *us* against *you* in the finals! Can you believe it?"

"That's *amazing*," said Duncan. He saw his mother turn away, still looking troubled. She always looks troubled, he reminded himself.

But over the next hour, Duncan kept thinking about panosis, that fatal disease, that disturbing and mysterious word.

Chapter Seventeen
YOU ARE GETTING VERY SLEEPY

As it turned out, Nate didn't even have to tell his father he had lost. As soon as Larry Saviano and Wendell Bruno saw him coming toward them, they knew.

"Our suffering will never end," Wendell muttered to his former partner. Wendell had shown up at the tournament that morning and had asked Larry if he could hang around with him during the last games. Larry, out of nostalgia for old times, had reluctantly agreed.

"Keep quiet, Wendell," said Larry now. "This is my *son* we're talking about. I don't want him to feel worse than he probably already does."

Nate slowly came over to them in the atrium and said, "I guess you figured it out, Dad, right?"

Larry nodded. "I guess I did. Unless this is some elaborate fake-out."

"No," said Nate. "Not this time."

"Well, I'm proud of you, son," Larry said stiffly. It was like an animatronic version of him talking. Nate knew his father was feeling many emotions right now, but pride probably wasn't one of them. Still, it was nice of him to pretend.

After a little while, Larry Saviano excused himself and walked away, followed by Wendell Bruno, who kept saying, "Larry, Larry, what are we going to do now?"

"Will you please leave me alone, Wendell?" Larry said. "I don't know what *we're* going to do now. But it's over, okay? *We'll* have to find a way to move on."

"I can't move on," said Wendell, and he removed his dark glasses. Behind them, he had been crying.

Nate was relieved when his mother and Dr. Steve and Eloise came over to say supportive things to him. "I am lucky to have you in the family," said Dr. Steve. "You're the best."

He and Nate's mother both put their arms around him. Nate impulsively lifted Eloise onto his shoulders, and she pulled at his long hair and screamed with happiness. Duncan and April joined them, too; those two still had so much adrenaline from having both made it to the finals that they didn't know what to do with themselves.

"I thought we had a real shot at winning," Nate explained to his mother and his stepfather. "Duncan here played PANOSIS, which was no good. But then, a turn later, Carl turned it into PASSION. It was amazing."

Dr. Steve wrinkled up his face. "Panosis?" he said. "That sounds like maybe you thought it was a disease of some kind, Duncan. You probably know that -osis—and -itis, too—is the suffix for certain diseases."

"It *is* a disease," Duncan said. "I'm positive."

"How do you spell it?" Dr. Steve asked, and Duncan spelled it out for him.

"No, Duncan, that's not a real disease," said Nate's stepfather. "I'm a doctor. I've memorized every disease from beriberi to elephantiasis. Let me put it this way: diseases are my two-letter words. I need to know them all in order to be good at what I do."

So now it was confirmed by an expert that panosis was definitely not real. Duncan wanted to ask his mother if she was positive she'd gotten the name of his father's disease right all these years, but he didn't have a chance to, because Lucy Woolery grabbed his arm. "Emergency meeting on the beach in five minutes," she said. "Be there."

"What do you mean?" Duncan asked. "A meeting about what?"

"I'll just say this: I saw how destroyed Nate's dad was after Nate and Maxie lost," Lucy said. "And I figured out a way I might be able to help them."

"Okay, I'll be there," said Duncan, though he had no idea what Lucy was talking about. Everything was puzzling today; nothing added up.

Five minutes later, when Duncan arrived at the beach, he took off his shoes and socks and walked in the sand. Soon his feet were coated, and they felt like breaded cutlets. But they felt good, too; they'd been sweating all day inside thick socks and sneakers. April waved to him, and Duncan walked over into the shade of a big striped beach umbrella, where several players had now gathered.

"What's this, an exorcism?" Carl Slater joked.

Duncan looked down at the sand. A big beach blanket had been laid out, and on top of it, Nate's father and his former Scrabble partner, Wendell Bruno, lay flat on their backs, side by side, both of them smiling self-consciously.

"Okay, let's get started," Lucy said. "We don't have a lot of time before the final round." She stood at the foot of the blanket, holding an electric toothbrush with a spinning, buzzing head.

Duncan turned to April to ask what was going on, but she shushed him. "Just watch," April said.

"Larry Saviano and Wendell Bruno," said Lucy in a voice

both serious and calm. "I want you to relax, and to keep your eyes on the spinning head of my toothbrush. Watch the bristles, watch the bristles. You are getting very sleepy . . ."

Larry and Wendell watched the toothbrush, which just seemed to vibrate. Duncan noticed that their eyes grew heavy; both grown men began to blink like two babies being rocked in a cradle.

Lucy was hypnotizing them.

Duncan remembered Lucy mentioning that she was an amateur hypnotist, but he'd had no idea that he would see her skill in action this weekend.

"Now you are both asleep," Lucy said to the men in that same strangely calm voice. "And you will stay asleep until I say you can wake up. While you sleep, I am going to tell you a story. You will listen to it, and you will experience the story as though it really took place exactly the way I tell it. And when you wake up, you will think about my story, and it will fill you with happiness. Do you understand?"

"I understand," murmured Wendell, though Larry said nothing.

"Okay, then here we go," said Lucy. "It's the winter of seventh grade, *twenty-six years ago*. You are two very smart twelve-year-old boys, and you have come all the way across the country to attend the Scrabble tournament. You are both really good players, and you're excited to be here. Aren't you excited, boys?"

"Yes," said Wendell in a voice that sounded different and young. "I am so excited I could burst my butt!"

"Yes, well, *that* wasn't awkward at all," Lucy said to the people watching. "How about you, Larry?" she asked. Nate's father slowly sat up and opened his eyes.

"Sorry," he said. "It's not working for me, Lucy. I tried, but I'm afraid I just couldn't fall into a trance."

"Oh," said Lucy, disappointed. "Too bad; I thought you were under. Just watch Wendell for now." She turned back to Wendell Bruno. "As I was saying . . . the six rounds have gone really well," she went on. "They've gone so well that you have made it all the way to the finals. The big game is thrilling. You are playing against two brainy girls, and you are beating them. The finals are almost over. You just need to hang on to your lead a little longer. The girls have picked the last tiles from the bag. Now they have seven on their rack, and they start moving them around, but it's your move. You make a nice play. You make . . . oh, let's say . . . FRONT. The F is on a double-letter square, and the whole word is on a double-*word* square. It's worth twenty-four points. The girls keep moving their tiles around, searching for a bingo, for that's the only way they can win."

"Oh no," murmured Wendell Bruno from his trance. "They're going to make ZYGOTES."

"Let's take a look at the letters on the other players' rack, okay?" said Lucy.

"Oh no, let's not," said Wendell. "I can't bear to look."

"Come on, it's okay," Lucy insisted gently. She began to say the letters aloud:

"G

T

Y

O

E

S . . ."

She paused here, and then she said the last letter:

"M."

"*M?*" said Wendell. "No, not M. It's Z. The other team has a Z on their rack."

"No," said Lucy in her hypnotist's voice. "In *my* version of the story, they have an M. Now, what bingo could they possibly make with those letters?"

"They *can't* make a bingo," said Wendell in childish wonder. "They don't have the Z for ZYGOTES. They would have to make . . . *MYGOTES*. But everyone knows that MYGOTES isn't a word."

Neither is PANOSIS, Duncan was reminded.

"You're right, they *can't* make anything good," Lucy continued. "So for their turn, they put down . . ." She paused dramatically. "MOSEY. For fourteen points."

"MOSEY?" said Wendell. "They only make MOSEY?"

"Yes. And now the game is just about over," said Lucy

Woolery. "It doesn't really matter where you place your tiles. So lay them down anywhere. Go on, lay them down."

Everyone watched as Wendell Bruno, a grown man lying on his back on a beach blanket, reached for invisible tiles and placed them on an invisible board in the air above him.

"That's sixteen points," said Wendell. "And we're out."

"Larry and Wendell," said Lucy. "You have won the tournament. You are the big winners! Enjoy this moment. Soon, Wendell, I am going to wake you up again, and when I do, I want you to *hold onto* the happiness you felt at winning the tournament. Whenever you think about the real event, I want you to understand that yes, you actually *did* lose, but I still want you to remember the story I told you. To remember the wonderful pleasure of winning. I want you to absorb it and make it feel as good and as valuable as if it happened. Do you understand?"

Wendell nodded. Lucy woke him up, and he sat up on the blanket beside Larry, completely disoriented.

"Why are we here? It's strange. I feel so relaxed," said Wendell, stretching his arms.

"Think about what happened back when you and I lost," said Nate's father.

"Okay," said Wendell. "I'm thinking about it."

"And is it okay?" Larry asked anxiously. "Can you handle the memory?"

"Why wouldn't I be able to handle it?" said Wendell. "It was a long time ago. We had a great time that weekend. It doesn't matter how the finals ended up. It was very exciting." Wendell looked happy; everyone could see that.

Moments later, Nate and his father stood at the shore together. "I wish Lucy had been able to hypnotize me, too," Larry said. "But I guess I need to deal with this on my own. There's no shortcut for me." He looked hard at Nate and said, "When I was your age, I wasn't half as brave."

"I'm not brave."

"Oh, yes, you are," said his father. "I watch you navigate the city—the streets, and all the people in them. I watch you navigate all this *technology* that you kids use; every day there's a new device, a new thing to learn, and yet you do it like it was nothing. I watch you navigate having two families, going back and forth all the time. And, of course, I watch you navigate having *me* as a dad." His voice broke slightly. "That can't be easy," Larry said. "Not easy at all. But I want it to be easier now, Nate. A lot easier." He paused. "I think it's great that you and Maxie played so well. And that you made new friends here. But I think we're done with Scrabble studying for a while, don't you? It's a terrific game. But there are other things you probably want to do, too."

"Yes," said Nate, "there are."

"From now on, I want you to do them, kid. All of them. Whatever you like."

Nate quietly began to cry. He couldn't even remember the last time he'd cried; it wasn't what he *did*. His father had given up his obsession at last. "Dad," he said softly. "I think you're going to be okay." And so am I, he thought. He and his father hugged, and then his father released him, and they walked back to join the others.

A little later, before the finals began, Wendell and Larry said good-bye to each other, probably for good. Wendell wasn't planning on sticking around to see who won the big game that afternoon. He said he didn't need to know. He was going back to his surfside cottage in Yakamee, where he planned to take a long nap, and then a walk by the ocean, and then maybe later he would invite someone to dinner. Cuddly the Iguana from Funswamp was nice, he told Larry. He'd always wanted to invite her over, but had never worked up the courage. Maybe today he finally would.

"Good-bye, Larry. Take it easy," said Wendell.

"Oh, I will. Good-bye, Wendell," said his former partner.

The crew from *Thwap!* TV had set up their cameras in the small room off the hotel ballroom where the final round would be filmed for live television. Tiny microphones were clipped to the four players' collars. Bill Prescott, the sports

237

announcer who gave blow-by-blows of the games that April's family often watched, paced the room, rehearsing what he was going to say on air.

"Scrabble," he said in his deep, syrupy voice. "One of America's best-loved board games. But did you know that this mild-mannered indoor game can be as fast-paced as soccer, as elegant as polo, or as brutal and bloody as football? Today we bring you live coverage from the Youth Scrabble Tournament in Yakamee, Florida, where two teams will be fighting to the finish for the national title . . . and *ten thousand dollars*."

Duncan sat in the corner by himself. He was so nervous that his whole body was quaking. The game would start in ten minutes, and he still didn't know how he would handle the problem of his fingertips. He realized that it would have been nice if he could tell himself he didn't care about winning. If he could tell himself he came here just to play.

But even though Duncan had come so far in a short period of time, and even though he knew how much fun it was to play your heart out, it would still feel interesting— no, it would still feel *great*—to win. He'd been thrilled each time he and Carl had won a game. He could barely imagine how it would feel to win the championship.

It would really be something to walk into Drilling Falls Middle School and hear people say, "Dorfman, you rock!"

It would really be something to give his mother the three thousand dollars.

And it would also really be something to know that Carl Slater didn't hate him anymore—and would never hate him again.

But if Duncan didn't use his fingertips when it mattered during the finals—and if Drilling Falls lost—Duncan would retreat back into himself. School would be agony again. Life would be, too.

The only way to guarantee a win would be for Duncan to simply give in and use his power, just as he had originally promised he would. Duncan told himself that April had already achieved what she'd hoped to here in Yakamee. In just a few minutes her whole family would watch her on *Thwap!* TV, and maybe it would finally sink into their brains that Scrabble was really a sport, and that April Blunt was amazing at it.

April didn't need to win in order to get that, Duncan thought as he sat in the corner. She had a lot less riding on winning than he did. He could use his fingertips in the finals, and April and Lucy would never know. Lucy, too, would be fine if they lost; Lucy was good at everything, so what did it really matter? She'd probably turn around and become the U.S. kid champion in Ping-Pong. April and Lucy would both be fine; he shouldn't have to feel guilty about them.

Everyone would go home tomorrow morning feeling

happy. So it was settled; he would put his hand into the bag and bring on the heat.

That's it, he told himself. *I've decided.* But the decision immediately made Duncan anxious. It unnerved him, and it felt wrong.

"Players, it's time to get set up at the table," said Dave Hopper.

Everyone took their places. A makeup woman came around with a powder puff, "to get rid of the shine," she said as she lightly patted it against Duncan's face. The powder made him cough, reminding him of the awful day when he'd shot the Smooth Moves cigarette ad at the Slaters' house. The cigarette ad was just one more unpleasant detail that awaited him in Drilling Falls.

In the final seconds before the live TV broadcast began, Carl turned to Duncan and said, "Dorfman, I have something to say to you."

"Okay," said Duncan.

"Make it right," said Carl in a low, intense voice.

"What?"

"You heard me. Make it right."

"What do you mean by that?" Duncan asked. "Tell me what you mean, Carl."

But it was too late to find out. The cameraman said, "Five, four, three, two, one . . ." and the red light on the camera snapped on.

Make it right, Duncan thought as he was thrust onto national TV. He tried to smile, but the white light was too bright. As soon as he looked down at the board, having just looked into the light, he couldn't see a thing. Everything appeared as its ghostly opposite. *Calm down,* Duncan told himself. *Just calm down. Don't have a freak-out.* Soon his vision returned to normal.

He took a few deep breaths and watched as Lucy Woolery drew the first tile from the bag. It was a C. Lucy smiled slightly, then quickly hid it.

Carl reached in and drew a W.

Duncan sat up straighter in his chair, his arms hugging his chest. The camera was trained on the board, and Duncan's eyes were, too. Out there in the ballroom on the other side of the wall, all 196 eliminated players sat in rows of banquet chairs, watching the game on an enormous screen. They'd all been given bags of popcorn and cans of soda, as though they were spending a relaxing afternoon at a movie.

For the four players in this little room, the final round was the opposite of relaxed. The game felt surreal to Duncan. The Oregonzos played their first word, then the Drilling Falls Scrabble Team played theirs. The words intersected and fed off one another; points were added to points. Both sides played with confidence.

Duncan saw Carl stare meaningfully at him from time to time, as if asking:

When are you going to use your fingertips?

But it wasn't necessary yet. Duncan and Carl chugged along, writing notes to each other on their pad, making good words and slightly less good words. Neither team had made a bingo yet. There were no blanks on the board. Anything could happen, Duncan knew, and probably many things would.

When the bag was half empty, Duncan reached in with his left hand and pulled out four tiles. He lined them up on the rack next to the three that were already there.

The letters, he saw, were astonishing.

Surely, on *Thwap!* TV right that second, the announcer was saying in a hushed and excited voice to the audience, "Folks, the Drilling Falls team has just drawn an incredible set of letters! Wow, baby, wow! Home run!"

Duncan and Carl were staring at this rack:

A

E

N

T

P

L

R

Carl gave Duncan a knowing look, and nodded. Then, on the pad of paper, Carl wrote:

Thank you, Dorfman.

Duncan realized that Carl had once again assumed that Duncan had deliberately selected these letters. Carl still didn't seem to remember that chance could also bring you a winning rack. Duncan didn't feel like letting Carl know that the tiles had been drawn the way anyone in any Scrabble game might have drawn them. Besides, there wasn't time for that right now. The clock was running down.

Both boys had seen the word PLANTER. But the problem was, Duncan realized after a second, there was nowhere to put it.

Ugh.

It was a classic homeless bingo. They looked and looked, searching the board for a place to hook a letter, perhaps the P at the start of the word, or the R at the end of it, but there was nothing.

"What are we going to do?" Carl said under his breath. Duncan cracked his knuckles in anxiety, then realized how loud it had probably sounded on TV.

He was frantic now, but also powerless. The letters simply did not fit. Then Duncan told himself to calm down and think. He knew, of course, that you could also add another letter to your own seven in order to make an *eight*-letter bingo. Was there any single letter on the board that could fit seven letters around it?

The A could do it.

The A was just sitting there, part of the word ARCH.

Duncan tried to figure out what eight-letter bingo he could possibly form around that A. He picked up a few tiles on his rack and moved them. With the A in the mix, he saw that he could make:

PRENATAL

He knew that word meant "before birth." Right now, thinking about it, the word made him feel *strange*. It was as if he was being hypnotized, as Lucy had hypnotized Larry Saviano's former partner, Wendell. He imagined himself as a tiny baby who hadn't even been born yet, floating inside his mother's womb. Caroline Dorfman and Duncan's father, Joe Wright, must have been scared but excited, knowing that they were going to have a baby.

Then Duncan moved the letters around some more. It was so peculiar, but they also scrambled to make:

PARENTAL

Now he imagined his young parents several months later, eagerly awaiting his birth. Maybe they went out and bought a crib for Duncan's room, and a mobile with ducks on it. Maybe they sang songs to him while he was still inside the womb. Surely Duncan's father couldn't wait to meet his son.

Duncan restlessly moved the letters again. This time they spelled out yet *another* word. It was:

PATERNAL

This word meant "having to do with fatherhood," and it made Duncan Dorfman push back a little in his chair. He thought of Joe Wright looking forward to becoming a father, but dying tragically of a rare disease before he ever had the chance.

It was too sad to believe, Duncan thought. It was so *incredibly sad* that his father had died of panosis before he was able to become paternal. Before he could hold little baby Duncan in his arms.

It was too sad to believe, Duncan Dorfman thought again. And then he realized that he actually *didn't* believe it.

He didn't believe it at all.

After all, PANOSIS had been no good; Dr. Steve had confirmed that it wasn't a real disease. Then why had Duncan's mother always told him that his father had died of panosis?

Maybe panosis was just a made-up word told to a child thoughtlessly, in a hurry, when he'd begun to ask his mother a lot of questions. And once she'd said it, she'd needed to stick to it:

"What did my dad die from?"

"What? Oh, your dad died from . . . panosis. Yes, it was very, very sad. Now listen, Duncan, I'm seeing an aura again. I think I need to go lie down. I've put a cheese sandwich for you on the table."

Duncan realized, too, that his mother's migraine

headaches had something in common. Each time she got one, she seemed to have just been thinking about or talking about Duncan's father. Yesterday, she'd told Duncan that her migraine had come on right after talking to Nate's father, Larry, about being a single parent.

Thinking about Duncan's father always caused Caroline Dorfman a lot of stress.

Why? he wondered. Why would it cause her so much stress?

Why would she need to make up the name of a fatal disease?

Why didn't any of this make sense?

In a way, Duncan knew, he had questioned the story about his father for some time. His mother had always been so *vague* about Joe Wright—what he was like, how long he had been sick with panosis. But Duncan had never wanted to bring it up and upset his fragile mother.

And then there had been all the whispered conversations she had at night with Aunt Djuna. *"I realize it's not perfect,"* she had told his great-aunt.

And Aunt Djuna had said, *"He deserves better."*

Yes, he deserved to know the truth. It was only now, during the finals of the Youth Scrabble Tournament, in front of a live TV audience, that Duncan could really concentrate on what the truth might be. Now, of all times, it came together and took on meaning.

PRENATAL . . .

PARENTAL . . .

PATERNAL . . .

The words were like a trail of clues, leading to a wild conclusion, perhaps a *wrong* one, but a conclusion nonetheless:

Duncan's father was alive.

He didn't even know he had fainted until he saw April's face above him, looking frightened. "Duncan?" she was saying. "Duncan? Are you okay?"

"I think so," he said, but he realized he was on the floor. This was like falling off a skateboard, but much stranger.

Someone helped him sit up and gave him a glass of water. The *Thwap!* TV announcer had cut to a commercial, and now the television crew was gathered around him, murmuring to themselves. A man with a headset came over and said, "Duncan, we've got a doctor coming in here in just a moment. He's Nate Saviano's stepdad."

"Oh, he's nice," said Duncan, "but I don't need a doctor. I'm fine now," he added, and it was actually, suddenly true.

"Are you sure?" asked the man nervously. "Because you fainted, you know."

"I know," said Duncan. "What's happening with the game?"

"Both of your timers are paused," the man said. "You'll

resume playing when you're ready. If you can't continue, we'll cut to a taped sporting event. Boxing, I think. Humboldt versus Suarez. Don't worry about it."

"I'm ready," said Duncan.

Make it right, Carl had warned him before the game started, and Duncan now knew how to do that. After he swore to all the adults around him that he was perfectly fine—that he had simply been overexcited because of the game—the players took their seats at the table again, and the red light of the TV camera came on.

The game resumed where it had left off. The bingo PATERNAL was selected and played by Duncan, and then it was April and Lucy's turn. Back and forth both teams went, and the game was tremendously close the whole way. Something needed to be done to pull Drilling Falls ahead. To win.

It was now or never.

Carl pushed the tile bag toward Duncan and whispered, "Here you go, dude. Do it for Drilling Falls."

Duncan reached his left hand into the opening of the velvet bag, his fingers fishing around inside. A new calm had settled over him.

Make it right, he thought. Duncan knew that he didn't want any more lies. He wanted only what was real. Yes, of course he wanted his team to win, but he wouldn't do it in some phony, cheater's way that would make him feel bad whenever he thought about it for the rest of his life.

Also, he wouldn't pretend to Carl that he had done it that way, either.

Make it *right*.

Duncan Dorfman took that phrase literally.

He removed his left hand from the bag. Making sure that Carl was watching, he plunged his right hand in instead.

"What are you doing?" mouthed Carl, practically hysterical. "This is *it*, man, this is the moment! Wrong hand, dude, wrong hand!"

Duncan calmly felt the tiles. None of them bloomed into hot life, of course; his right hand had never possessed that skill. He felt absolutely nothing on those plastic squares. Their surfaces were cool and flat, and Carl could tell this by Duncan's expression.

"You know what you are?" said Carl. "You're a nothing. You're just . . . Lunch Meat." He hissed the words close to Duncan's ear, which grew red, as if it were on fire. *"Lunch Meat,"* Carl repeated, taunting him, and the cameras and the microphone picked up this moment, too.

Now everyone watching this show on TV would know Duncan's nickname, and they would call him that whenever they teased him.

But when he pulled the letters out and looked at them, he immediately stopped thinking about being teased by Carl or anyone else. He saw that, by pure luck, the tiles happened to be pretty good. He had drawn the Z, among other letters, and the board was still open. Duncan sensed that April and Lucy simply wouldn't be able to catch up now.

It was a mixed feeling. Triumph, along with a touch of sadness and regret. Duncan looked at April Blunt's eyes across the board, but they didn't reveal a thing. She seemed to be just watching the game carefully, as curious as anyone about how it would turn out. She could handle what happened next, which didn't mean she wouldn't be disappointed. But she and Lucy would indeed be okay. After all, everyone said, it was only a game.

Moments later, as if in a daze, Duncan laid down the last of the Drilling Falls team's tiles, and he and Carl won by 28 points.

They all shook hands across the board, the camera catching every moment. Duncan Dorfman and Carl Slater, from the town of Drilling Falls, Pennsylvania, became the new champions of the Youth Scrabble Tournament, with only forty-one seconds left on their clock.

Someone opened the door to the ballroom. As Duncan and Carl were led through, they could hear the cheering.

PART THREE

Chapter Eighteen
MAKING IT RIGHT

Later, after the ceremony at which the big check and the trophy were handed to the winners, after the applause and the interviews with TV news shows and websites and newspapers and call-in satellite radio shows, Duncan Dorfman was wiped out. He had never had a day as big as this one, and he knew he would probably never have one as big again. He had come from nothing and nowhere and won everything. Or at least, thirty percent of it.

An interviewer with a British accent had asked him, "Duncan, why did Carl refer to you as . . . Luncheon Meat, I believe?"

"Lunch Meat," Duncan said.

"It's just a friendly nickname," Carl said quickly. "A name that American kids sometimes call their good friends."

Carl was piling the lies on thick. And good friends, the two of them? Hardly.

Now Duncan Dorfman lay on his back on a whale-shaped float in the middle of the pool on the roof of the Grand Imperial Hotel, holding a glass of fruit punch and looking up at the dimming sky at the end of the day. All around him, kids from the tournament splashed and shrieked. There was Nate Saviano, one-half of the third-place team. He and Maxie had split the twenty-five-hundred-dollar prize. Though very few people knew this, on his way out of the ceremony, Nate had walked over to the Wranglers, Tim and Marie. They still wore their giant cowboy hats, though the edges looked a little wilted after the long and difficult weekend.

"How'd you do?" Nate had asked them. "Where'd you place, finally?"

"Ninety-seventh," said Marie.

"Oh," said Nate. "Okay. Well, not bad."

"That's right, it's not. We hope we get to come back next year," Tim said.

Nate looked around to make sure they had privacy. "Listen, guys," he said quietly. "I want you to have my prize

254

money. I'm going to send it to you. Use it for your airfare and expenses next year." The Wranglers just stared, pop-eyed.

"You're *giving us* your money, Nate?" Tim said.

"Yeah, I am," said Nate. "I want you to have it. It's yours."

Now Nate was swimming under the water like a seal, feeling truly free for the first time in a long while. Maxie saw him and jumped into the water with a wild splash, landing right beside him.

"Yo!" she cried.

From his whale float, Duncan watched Nate and Maxie laugh and joke around. They seemed a tiny bit older than everyone else, and it was as if they shared so much. The whole boyfriends-and-girlfriends thing was going to start pretty soon, Duncan knew. They would all become teenagers, and everything was going to change. But everything was *always* changing; he already knew that.

"Marco!" Duncan heard Tim shout from the other side of the pool.

"Polo!" Marie shouted back.

Someone swam up to the whale and said, "Hey, Duncan."

It was Carl, his hair slicked back with water. Ever since the finals today, the two of them hadn't really spoken. They'd posed together, and they'd been interviewed together, but they hadn't been alone face-to-face. What had happened in the final game was still obviously a tense subject.

But now, here they were in the pool. No one was nearby; this was just between them.

"Hey," said Duncan cautiously. He didn't want Carl Slater to start up with him again. He just didn't have the energy for it. "I know what you're going to say," he said to Carl. "'How could you have used your *right* hand like that in the final round?' 'How could you have been *so stupid* to almost blow everything we worked so hard for?' 'How could you be such a *Dwarfman*, such a *Lunch Meat?*'"

"No," Carl interrupted sharply. "I wasn't. And I'll never call you Lunch Meat again. I told you to make it right, didn't I? I meant, do the right thing. I couldn't keep up with you anymore. You were *way* beyond me. It all made me crazy; it made me so mad, but I figured I had to let you do what you needed to do. And I hoped that maybe if you did the thing that *you* thought was right, it would work out. And despite everything—you know, the way it all happened, and the way I acted—I guess it did."

"Thanks," was all Duncan said.

"I'm sorry I was such a jerkface all weekend. I shouldn't have pushed you. I shouldn't have been sarcastic. I shouldn't have called you names during the last game. I guess I'm totally competitive, no matter what I'm doing.

I've always been that way," Carl admitted. "When I was, like, four, playing Pin the Tail on the Donkey, I tripped this little girl at her own birthday party so I could be next in line. And then I *still* didn't pin the tail in the right place. I pinned it on her grandma instead. So I had a tantrum."

"And you had another one today," said Duncan.

"Yeah. But listen. I also wanted to say that I'm going to split the money fifty-fifty. I was thinking about it, and I decided it's only fair."

"Really?" Duncan said, surprised.

"Really."

Duncan sensed that he would never be Carl's Scrabble partner again. He couldn't exactly trust what Carl said. Even now, was Carl being entirely honest in his apology? Duncan wasn't sure. He was too overwhelmed to think it all through; he had much bigger issues on his mind now, disturbing questions that had been raised as he'd scrambled and unscrambled words in that final game, and which wouldn't go away on their own. But he was glad Carl had volunteered to split the money.

In the water, with wet hands, the boys shook on the deal.

The day was fading fast, and from the lounge chairs where Duncan and Carl now sat side by side in the silence of their uneasy truce, they saw a small airplane forming skywriting. "Look at that," said Carl. "Writing in the sky." He smiled slyly. "Or maybe you don't even have to look," he said.

"What?"

"You could probably just *feel* that skywriting."

"Carl, no."

"Come on, Duncan. For old time's sake," Carl Slater said. "One last time. No one's around. Let's see how far you can take this skill of yours. We've never really put it to the test, have we?"

Duncan hesitated. He had never tested his power in any unusual ways. Would he actually be able to feel letters in the *distance*, his fingers seeming to be on top of them, but not actually *touching* them?

He and Carl walked to the railing at the edge of the roof, and Carl wrapped a towel around Duncan's head as a blindfold. Duncan put his hand up to the sky where the skywriting was forming. He waited a moment, trying to make it happen. And sure enough, his fingers turned hot, and the heat blossomed in them, and then he actually felt the fluffy cold swirl of the skywriting, exactly as if he was touching it. As if he was right up there in the sky.

He read aloud:

"THE GRAND IMPERIAL HOTEL CONGRATU-LATES THE YST WINNERS!"

He kept his hand over the letters and felt them as they evaporated. It was the strangest feeling ever. Duncan opened his eyes.

"Whoa," said Carl. "Incredible. You frighten me, man! I mean . . . who are you?"

It was a very good question.

"Wake up, kid," Nate's father said in Nate's ear the next morning. "We've got a plane to catch." Larry Saviano was smiling. He was actually *happy*. Not only had he made his peace with his loss of many years ago, and vowed to be a different kind of father to Nate, but last night, at the hotel bar, Larry Saviano and Caroline Dorfman had had a long conversation, and they'd said they would stay in touch. Maybe Larry and Nate would even take a drive to Pennsylvania when the weather got nicer.

A second good thing had also happened to Larry. Walking back to the hotel from dinner last night, two college kids had come up to him. One of them said, "Aren't you Lawrence Saviano?"

"Yes," he said. "Why?"

"We read your *Zax* books," said the other one. "We recognized your picture from the back. You're like . . . brilliant!"

"I am?" said Larry.

"Oh yeah," said the first one. "We're students at Yakamee U. You're getting a pretty big following on our campus. Are there going to be any more books in the series, Mr. Saviano?"

"Yes!" Nate's father cried in delight. "As of this minute, plenty more."

Now, in the hotel room in the morning, Larry sat humming as he pulled on his socks. Nate had arranged to meet Maxie in the hall; he went out with his skateboard and waited for her, and there she was. Her hair was spikier than usual from sleep.

Nate and Maxie slapped hands in the air, and their hands stayed put for an extra half second. Then Maxie said, "Let's have one more ride before we go."

They walked together down the long hall. Nate thought about the little skate park across the street from the school, and how surprised everyone would be on Monday morning when he showed up there again. And this time, when they said to him, "You're back?" he would tell them yes, he was back.

"I'm just warning you," said Maxie as they headed for the elevator. "The new math teacher is about a hundred and fifty years old."

"I can handle it," said Nate.

"And she gives pop quizzes every nanosecond."

That was supposed to be a warning, too, but all Nate could think as he and Maxie went outside and got on their boards was that for some reason he looked forward to those quizzes.

He picked up speed, and Maxie kept pace beside him.

In the Blunt hotel suite that morning, April's mother went around to everyone in the family who lay sprawled or curled on beds and couches and rollaway cots, saying to them, "Time to go home, team."

Slowly, the team opened its eyes.

In room 1504, where the Slaters were staying, Mrs. Slater shook her slumbering son, saying, "CARL, PICK UP YOUR TROPHY AND LET'S GET READY TO CHECK OUT. DO YOU HEAR ME, CARL? DO YOU HEAR ME?"

Up in room 1830, Duncan awakened and yawned. It took him a few moments, but when he saw the giant check leaning against the dresser, he remembered that he and Carl had won the tournament. "How does it feel?" people had been asking him the afternoon and evening before. "How does it feel to be the winner?"

"It feels incredible," he'd told them. But after a while, the answer didn't seem completely accurate.

His mother had hugged him and cried after she came rushing up to him in the ballroom moments after the game ended. They were interviewed together, and he heard

261

her say, "I am so proud of Duncan, I can't tell you. It's just the two of us, and I know it hasn't always been easy for him."

Duncan had stood there smiling stiffly. He was happy, although every few minutes, the same thoughts returned:

What about my father?

Is he really alive, or am I jumping to an insane conclusion?

He was no longer at all certain, but still he had to know. He needed to find the right time to confront his mother. Yesterday after the finals hadn't worked, and this morning wouldn't work either, because they were going to have to hurry up and pack their things in order to catch the flight back to Drilling Falls. He would ask her at home.

"Wake up, Mom," Duncan said. "It's time to go."

At the checkout desk in the lobby of the Grand Imperial Hotel, the kids from the tournament said their good-byes. Lucy Woolery found herself crying as she wrote out her e-mail address many times. "Will you all *please* come and visit April and me in Portland?" she said. "I'm an only child, and I have plenty of room."

"And also please come down to Butterman, Georgia," said Josh of the Evangelical Scrabblers. "We've got a pond with a rope swing that goes all the way across."

Nate slung the ratty little Scaly stuffed animal from

Funswamp over his shoulder. Stuffing was already leaking out from the seam. Nate was going to take the alligator home and keep it for a few weeks, then it would spend a few weeks at Maxie's place, and go back and forth. "Come visit New York City," Nate said to everyone. "Maxie and I will take you on the subway, and to Chinatown for soup dumplings."

"But we'll also take you to P.S. five eighty-five," said Maxie. "There's a great skate park across the street. I mean, it's not *great*, but we like it."

"You should all come to Drilling Falls, Pennsylvania," Duncan said. "We've got freezing temperatures and a Thriftee Mike's Warehouse superstore, and I've got a house that smells of yams."

"I'll visit you, Duncan," April said to him seriously.

April knew that all of them would stay in touch, and that they would play online Scrabble games with one another probably a lot more than they should. She was planning to send an e-mail to Duncan that very night, when she got back to Oregon. She would write:

Hi, Duncan,

Long time no see. How does it feel to be national champion? Was Carl annoying on the plane? Did he steal your little bag of pretzels? Did he try to steal your oxygen mask?

Remember Funswamp? I can't wait to go back. (JUST
KIDDING!)

        Bye for now,

        April B. (member of 2nd-place winning team)

P.S. How's your maimed knee?

Duncan joked with everyone now about the place
where he lived, but he really was eager to get back to his
great-aunt's house. He needed to sit somewhere quiet with
his mother and finally get her to tell him the whole truth
about his father.

In the lobby, everyone except Nate swore they would
return to the YST a year from now. ("I promise to possibly
return as a special adviser and spectator," Nate said. "But
that is IT.") Some of the girls hugged some of the boys. The
Word Gurrrls went around giggling inappropriately, and
the Wranglers ran around shouting good-bye to everyone
multiple times.

"Duncan, you'll have to come back and defend your
championship," said Maxie.

"Okay, sure," said Duncan, although he knew that if
he did come back, it would be with a different partner. But
Carl would want to come back as well; maybe Drilling Falls
could send two teams.

They all traveled in taxis and shuttle buses and vans

to the Yakamee Airport, going past Funswamp, which, April saw from the back of the van that the Blunts and the Woolerys were sharing, had a sign out front that read: CLOSED FOR REPAIRS. It had been closed ever since the Lazy Swamp Ride had gotten sabotaged, and who knew when it would reopen again. April sat beside Liz, who had a new interest in her sister. April and Liz were looking at a spreadsheet of Scrabble games that had been played at various tournaments around the country.

"Check out these kids from Nevada," Liz said. "They're only *nine*. Excellent win record. Next year, they'll be old enough for the YST. I bet they come here and give you a run for your money."

"Well, Lucy and I have to start practicing again," said April. "It's never too early to think about next year."

"We should come up with a new practice schedule," said Lucy, who was sitting in the middle seat with her parents. "Maybe we could meet after school—"

"No more talk about practicing from any of you!" April's mother called from the front seat. "I am putting a temporary ban on all sports, Scrabble included!" (Although the following day, when everyone was settled back at home, Mrs. Blunt would start a new photo album, completely devoted to April and Scrabble.)

At the airport, April and Lucy sat alone in the terminal by the wall of windows, watching planes take off and land. They would have a long flight all the way across the continent to Portland, Oregon, leaving this sunny climate and heading back to that place of frequent rain that they called home.

"So, Flink," said Lucy, "we did okay, didn't we?"

"Yes, Curnish, we did," said April. "Second place is pretty good." They had won five thousand dollars and the respect of the entire Blunt family. "I have to pee," she suddenly said.

"You and Tim both," Lucy said.

"I'll be right back," said April. She started to walk across the concourse toward the women's room. Much later, she would wonder if she'd really had to go to the bathroom at all, or whether something else, something unexplainable, had gotten her out of her seat.

Rounding the corner at that moment came a big group of kids. Some of them wore T-shirts that read JUNIOR GYMNASTS. Others wore jackets that read WASHINGTON STATE ATHLETICS; these were the Seattle entrants in the gymnastics competition that had been taking place in Ballroom B of the hotel, one flight up, all weekend. There had been no overlap between the gymnasts and the Scrabblers, and none of them had met.

April saw that one of the gymnasts, a girl, wore a blue T-shirt with red letters that read SEATTLE MARINERS.

The words on the T-shirt did a little dance in April's

brain, the way words sometimes did. Usually, she just scrambled and unscrambled letters, and that was that. But now, the blue T-shirt reminded her of that other T-shirt belonging to the boy at the motel pool all those years ago— the T-shirt that had read SETTLE MARS.

With a shocked laugh, April finally understood. Back at the motel pool three years earlier, the boy's T-shirt had been briefly *creased* from wearing it in the water. The reason April hadn't remembered the phrase SETTLE MARS was that the shirt hadn't said that.

It had said SEATTLE MARINERS.

The vertical creases in the shirt had hidden some of the letters when her father took the photo. The A in SEATTLE wasn't visible, and neither was the INER in MARINERS.

For a few seconds it had read:

SE TTLE MAR   S

Except the creases had pushed the letters together, so it seemed more like: SETTLE MARS

April had always been bored by the names of sports teams, and so she hadn't remembered what was really written on his T-shirt. But now she did remember, and her heart began to race. She was standing in the airport near a group of gymnasts from Seattle, and she couldn't help but wonder something further. She stood very still and looked around.

What were the chances?

As she stood there, a boy walked toward her, eating one

of those pretzels that people ate in airports and nowhere else. He was tall, with brownish hair and a serious face. He wore a white T-shirt that didn't have anything written on it at all. He had an athletic bag over his shoulder, because he was with that group of kid gymnasts from Seattle. He looked at April, and then he looked at her again. She looked right back at him. She knew that it was him, after all this time. He wasn't skinny anymore, but all at once she remembered his face.

It was the boy from the motel pool.

He lived in Seattle, which wasn't very far from Portland, but April had had no idea, because she'd been confused by the photograph in her family's album. SETTLE MARS meant nothing to him. He just liked the Mariners, his local team.

The boy walked up to April, finishing his pretzel, and he said, "Wait, we know each other, right?"

"I think so," she said, but the words barely got out.

"You're that girl," he said. "The one that I met."

April could only nod. "At the motel pool," she finally said.

The boy smiled and said, "SOMERSAULT. Am I right?"

"Yes," she said. "That's it."

SOMERSAULT was the solution to the anagram of ROAST MULES. He'd figured it out sometime over the past three years, and she was astonished that he'd remembered. But this whole experience was astonishing.

"I was actually here in Florida this weekend for a word thing," April said. "A Scrabble tournament."

"How'd you do?" he asked.

"Second place."

"Nice. I was here for gymnastics. My group did so-so, but we're going to come back next year." He paused, then said, "You know, it's funny. But that day at the pool?"

"I taught you Scrabble," said April. "That's what you were going to say, right?"

"No, I was going to say that you sort of got me moving around that day. Your family was out at a baseball game or something, I think. You went in the water, and you got me to go in, too, which was sort of a big deal for me. And we joked around a lot, and when your family got back, your brother did this somersault into the pool—"

"Right. That's what made me give you the anagram," said April.

"And I went back home," he said, "and I thought how great it would be to be able to do stuff like that. Swimming. Somersaults. Physical stuff. I started doing gymnastics at school. Maybe it was sort of because of that day."

An announcement came over the loudspeaker for April's flight to Portland. She had only just *found* him, and now she had to leave. "Listen, I've got to go," she said. "But here's my e-mail." She quickly wrote it down on a little scrap of paper, and he wrote his down, and they swapped.

His name was Jake Kennelly, and he was thirteen years old. *Jake.* That was his name, after all this time. He'd always been Jake Kennelly from Seattle, but she hadn't known it.

"Well, take it easy, April," Jake said.

"I have to ask you something," she suddenly said. "Did you keep playing Scrabble?"

Jake Kennelly shook his head. "No," he said. "I don't think I've played it since. I've been pretty busy with the gymnastics team, and school."

Some of his friends called to him that it was time to go. He said to April, "We'll be in touch," and then he was gone.

In the distance, April saw Lucy standing very still in the middle of the concourse, watching the scene. April was certain that Lucy had already figured out who she had been talking to.

"Don't tell me, Flink," Lucy would say.

Then April would tell her.

Chapter Nineteen
THE TRUTH ABOUT DUNCAN DORFMAN

On the plane ride from Florida to Pennsylvania, Duncan kept a pair of earbuds in his ears, listening to the music channels that the airline offered. He wasn't in the mood for music—he wasn't like Nate, who often had music on—but he just couldn't deal with his mother yet. The questions he needed to ask her couldn't be asked on a plane.

Once they started talking, though, and once he demanded the truth from her, he knew that he would have to tell *her* the truth, too. Soon she would learn why Carl had asked him to the tournament; soon she would learn about the ad for Smooth Moves cigarettes.

What Duncan hadn't counted on was how soon the ads would be up. Coming home from the airport, riding over the bumpy, slushy roads of Drilling Falls, the taxi stopped at a red light downtown, and that was when Duncan saw it. On the side of a bus shelter he made out the words SMOOTH MOVES, and below them was a photograph of two boys playing a board game.

Duncan was horrified. But as he peered through the frosted, ice-crackled glass of the taxi window, he saw that something had been done to the ad. Frantically, he rubbed the window with his fingertips until the frost cleared. Someone had vandalized the ad; with thick magic marker, a cartoon face had been drawn over Duncan's face, so that his identity was hidden. In the place of Duncan Dorfman's face was the face of an alien with antennae.

An alien who looked a lot like one of Andrew Tanizaki's drawings.

Andrew, Duncan understood, must have seen the ad when it had been put up this weekend, and he had gone downtown and drawn over it as a way to protect Duncan. He had suspected that Duncan would be ashamed to be in this ad, and so he'd done what he could in the freezing cold. Duncan hoped he'd at least worn gloves.

He could just picture Andrew Tanizaki out there on a

sleeting gray afternoon, looking around to make sure that no one saw him, then drawing over the ad.

He would have to find a way to thank him.

At home, Aunt Djuna flung the front door of the house wide open. "I watched you on the TV!" she cried as Duncan and his mother came up the porch steps. "I've never watched that little TV you brought when you moved in, but my neighbor Mrs. Gunvalson showed me how you get it to work. There are hundreds of channels, did you know that?"

"Yes," said Duncan. "I did."

"One of them is just about vegan cooking! Anyway, you were magnificent, Duncan."

Inside, he realized that the house was infused with a surprisingly inviting smell.

"Aunt Djuna, what is that?" Duncan asked. "Chocolate?"

Aunt Djuna smoothed down the edges of her green sweater. "Well, yes," she said. "I thought I would make a treat in honor of our big Scrabble champion. Do you like brownies?"

"Very much," said Duncan.

"I'm so glad," said Aunt Djuna. "Because I baked four trays."

It wouldn't be until much later, of course, after dinner was over and dessert had been put out on china plates, that

Duncan discovered that Aunt Djuna's brownies were made at least partly of yam. The dampness and texture and the little threads of orange color and bits of peel gave it away. But still he ate them, because it was only polite, and she was an extremely kind and generous person, and anyway, they weren't bad.

It also wasn't until much later that Caroline Dorfman appeared in the doorway of Duncan's room and said, "Hey, you. Have a second?"

He had been arranging some objects in his tiny room: the certificate from the tournament, and the score sheets from the different games, and Andrew Tanizaki's good-luck drawing, all of which he had carefully taped up on the wall over the bed.

Duncan looked up, surprised. He'd been meaning to work up the courage to confront his mother, but the time still hadn't been right. He worried that she would get a migraine. He worried that she would burst into tears when he asked her what he needed to ask. He worried most of all that she would tell him he was wrong.

But here she was, confronting *him*. She came into his room and shut the door behind her. The place was so small that they stood only inches from each other. "Duncan," she said. "I have a feeling that you were confused about some things this weekend."

Duncan couldn't meet her eyes. "What do you mean?"

"When you fainted during the game, I had the sense that . . . it was for an emotional reason. Am I right?"

"Maybe," he said.

"Wheels were turning in your head," said his mother. "I could almost see them on the big screen."

"It was that obvious?"

"To me it was," she said. "Earlier, you'd asked me about panosis, and why it was no good." Duncan nodded, and now he looked at her again. "You seemed suspicious about the trigger for my migraines," she went on. "I love you so much, Duncan, and I've gone around and around in my head about this. I've tortured myself thinking about it. I've talked about it endlessly with Aunt Djuna. She was there in the beginning, you know."

"Go on," was all he could say.

"You probably think I'm a bad person, lying to you like that," she said. "I just didn't know what else to do. I wanted to protect you. Aunt Djuna thought it was a very bad idea. She said you deserved better than that, and she's right."

"He's alive?" Duncan asked, cutting her off.

His mother didn't say anything. She didn't say, *"Are you crazy?"* or, *"That's ridiculous,"* or, *"Is who alive?"* Finally she nodded. "Yes," she said. "He is."

Duncan took a breath, and he felt himself trembling. "Is his name even Joe Wright?"

"No," she said quietly.

"How could you have lied to me all these years, Mom?"

"Because he asked me to," said his mother, in tears now, throwing her hands up in the air. "I'm very ashamed of myself, but honestly, I didn't know what else to do. He and I were so young when I found out I was pregnant with you. We were still teenagers. But I knew that if I was going to become your mom, then I'd have to grow up. But he couldn't do that."

"Why not?" asked Duncan.

"He knew, even before you were born, that he would be a bad father. He wasn't done being a boy himself. That was why I liked him originally, I think. He was boyish and fun. As far as I can tell, he *still* isn't done being a boy. I would have liked to marry him and give family life a try, but he said he couldn't handle it. He didn't want you to grow up thinking he had abandoned you—it wasn't *you* he felt he was abandoning, just the *idea* of you, if that makes any sense—so he asked me to make something up. I hated it, but I knew it would be years before the question would ever arise, so I agreed. My parents were no help; they were too shocked that I was having a baby. I moved away from Drilling Falls and went to Michigan, where you were born. Aunt Djuna wrote me every day, and she came out to visit whenever she could. She was so kind, and she helped me start a new life with you, away from here. And that worked for a very long time. You were a wonderful baby, Duncan, and a marvelous little boy. The first time you asked me what your dad had died of—until then, I'd been vague about it—I was caught up short, and I made up something on the spot. I came up with 'panosis' because of Peter Pan. A disease of someone who doesn't want to grow up."

"I can't believe this," said Duncan. "I CAN'T BELIEVE THIS!" he said again, and he realized he was shouting, the way Nate Saviano sometimes did. It felt surprisingly good. He had barely known what his voice sounded like when it came out of him at such a high volume.

"I know, honey, I know. It's a big shock. A big betrayal. Not a day has passed when I haven't felt bad about it. Can you see why I did it, and maybe start to forgive me?" she asked. "I'll understand if you can't."

He looked at her. There she was, the same person as ever. Her hair was blond and pulled back, and her eyes were blue. She was still his mother, his mom, the person who had raised him single-handedly. That hadn't changed, and wasn't going to.

Three seconds passed. "Yeah," he said. "I forgive you, Mom."

"Thank you, Duncan." The conversation seemed to be coming to a close, but then she said, "One more thing. I know you think I responded strangely when you showed me that power of yours back in the fall. That funny fingertip thing; do you remember what I'm talking about?"

"Yes," Duncan said faintly. One of these days, when he was brave enough, he would tell her all *his* secrets. But not now.

"The reason I was so worried about anyone else seeing it was that, after I lost my job in Michigan and we had to move back here, I just wanted to make sure we didn't call too much attention to ourselves in town. I didn't want people talking, bringing up the past. Mostly, I didn't want *him* getting involved. I really appreciate that you respected my wishes and never showed your power to anyone else."

There was a pause. "He's *here*?" Duncan said. "My father's here in Drilling Falls?" Duncan's mother nodded. "Who is he?" Duncan asked quietly.

His mother took a breath and wiped her eyes with her sleeve. "Your father," she said with a regretful little smile, "is Thriftee Mike."

Duncan and his mother sat in Aunt Djuna's squirrel-colored living room and talked until midnight, and she answered as many of his questions as she could. "Am I anything like him?" Duncan wanted to know.

"Well, neither of you is particularly tall, and you actually have similar hair," she said. "But beyond that, no, I don't think you have much in common. You're a serious, thoughtful person, Duncan, and he's just . . . a child. He's more of a child than you are, in fact. No, I'll go out on a limb here and say I don't think you have anything in common at all. Which is a good thing, believe me," she said.

They sat by the light of the glued-tail mermaid lamp. His mother had cried so much that her eyes looked like two boiled things. Duncan tried to make her feel better, and he even told her that he wanted to give her the five thousand dollars that he'd won in the tournament, but she brushed away the idea.

"Thank you, honey, that's generous of you, but I can't accept it," she insisted. "We'll get our own place eventually, I swear. We'll figure it out. Hold on to that money. You're going to need it." His mother finally yawned and said it was time for bed. "We can keep talking about this," she said. "I'm sure, someday, you'll even want to meet him, and then we'll have to find out if he's willing. Not that I think you'd get much out of it. As I said, he's entirely different from you."

A little later, after his mother had gone to sleep, Duncan sat up in his narrow bed, hugging his knees. His right knee still looked disgusting. He'd taken off the bandage in the shower that evening and was surprised to see how impressively ugly the gash was. Probably it would leave a scar. For the rest of his life, he would remember where it had come from. *The time I went flying off a skateboard*. Or, more to the point, *the first time I ever went on a skateboard.*

He longed to ride a skateboard again. Maybe he would take a little money from his winnings and buy himself one; there was a store in downtown Drilling Falls, right beside the pizza place. Duncan was very tired now, but his knee was aching and his mind was humming, and he knew he wouldn't be able to sleep at all. He had to go to school in the morning, and he would be a wreck.

As he lay wide awake, there was soft knocking on his door. Duncan was surprised to see Aunt Djuna standing in the hall in her nightgown, the green sweater draped over her shoulders as always.

"I saw the light under your door," she said. "I wondered if you needed anything."

"Oh, no thanks, Aunt Djuna," Duncan said. "The brownies were good. But I'm pretty full."

"I didn't mean brownies," Aunt Djuna said. "I meant a ride."

She had heard the entire conversation earlier between Duncan and his mother, Aunt Djuna explained as she drove him in the night down Main Street. She drove fast and dangerously; he worried that pieces of her little old car were going to fall off in the street. The car had a faulty heater, too, and Duncan was freezing as he sat beside her.

"I listened to what your mother said to you," Aunt Djuna said. "I'm sorry I eavesdropped, but in another way I'm not sorry one bit. You know, I was there years and years ago, when your mother was a teenager and first met Michael Scobee. I watched her fall in love with him. And when she found out she was pregnant, I was the one she came to talk to. Her own parents didn't want to hear. She's always been a brave woman, going through everything on her own. She had to grow up overnight."

"I know."

"It wasn't right of her to lie to you. But she always said to me, 'Djuna, if you know a better way, please tell me.' I called Michael Scobee and got him to give her a job at the superstore this fall, after she lost her own job in Michigan. I love your mother to pieces, Duncan—she is my favorite niece—but I politely disagree with some of the things she said to you about him. I figured," she said, "that you needed to find out some things for yourself. I know she told you that maybe you'd want to meet him 'someday.' But Duncan, you're twelve years old. To a twelve-year-old, the only good 'someday' is today."

Duncan knew that Thriftee Mike often came to his superstore at night when no one was there but the security guards. He went through the books and took care of business, which he wasn't comfortable doing during the day when his employees were around.

"The chances are fairly high that you can see him tonight," Aunt Djuna said as she drove.

"But how will we get in?" Duncan asked. "It's not like they're going to open the front door just because I knock on it and say, 'Let me in! I'm your son!'"

Aunt Djuna turned to him and laughed, taking her eyes off the road a little too long. "That's why I brought this with me," she said, and she reached into the pocket of her green sweater and took out a card. It said EMPLOYEE ID, and on it was a picture of Duncan's mother, staring red-pupiled at the camera. "I got this from your mother's purse after she finally conked out." Aunt Djuna pulled into the parking lot of Thriftee Mike's, parked the car sideways across the handicapped spot, and killed the lights. "Here we go," she said.

Duncan swiped the card into the card-reader at the employees' entrance just as easily as he had swiped the hotel key in the door lock of his room at the Grand Imperial. The door opened now, permitting entry. He realized that he didn't feel nervous, just *strange*. He and his great-aunt walked down a short hallway until they were in the main part of the store, which appeared dim and ghostly in the nighttime. Duncan could make out the giant bins of items in the enormous space. He saw electric pencil sharpeners; he saw dental floss and containers of microwavable artificial-shrimp-flavored ramen noodles. He and his great-aunt walked along the gleaming linoleum until they reached a door that read: ABSOLUTELY PRIVATE. DO NOT ENTER UNDER ANY CIRCUMSTANCES.

Aunt Djuna nodded. Duncan paused, walked up to the door, and knocked.

Within seconds, a security guard appeared. His name tag read I'M THRIFTEE TODD. When he saw Duncan, he said, "How the heck did you get in here?" He spoke a few words into his walkie-talkie, his other hand moving lightly onto the gun in his holster.

"The child would like to see Mr. Scobee," said Aunt Djuna. "We thought he might be here."

"He's not," said the security guard, looking back and forth between the boy and the woman, unsure of what to make of the situation.

"Oh, come on, Todd," she said, reading his name tag. "It's late, and I'm old. Please don't keep us waiting."

"Who are you?" asked the guard, looking straight at Duncan.

Duncan paused, and then he said, "I'm Thriftee Duncan."

The security guard gave a little snort. "Clever. Just a minute," he said, and he shut the door in their faces. Soon the door opened again, and the guard said, "He'll see you. I have no idea why."

Duncan and his great-aunt walked through the messy business offices. The guard opened an inner door, motioning them inside, and they walked in. That led to a huge, deep office; in the midst of all the fluorescent light and plastic around it, the office was luxurious, paneled and dark. A fish tank bubbled quietly along the length of one wall. In the distance was a desk, and at the desk sat a man.

Aunt Djuna and Duncan walked across the deep carpet until they stood right in front of the desk, and the man behind it stood up. He wasn't very tall. He had a face similar to Duncan's, though wider and more closed. His hair was wavy and a little wild, the same shade as Duncan's hair. He was slightly thick-chested like Duncan, too, and he wore jeans and a mustard-yellow shirt.

"You're Caroline's kid," said Thriftee Mike.

Duncan nodded.

Thriftee Mike nodded, too. "I assumed we'd meet at some point. I just didn't know it would be now, in the middle of the night, with no warning. Hello, Djuna. You're looking well."

"Not really, but hello, Mike."

"I suppose," Thriftee Mike said to Duncan, "your mother sent you? She's been remarkably restrained up until now, living here so discreetly this fall. Insisting on not taking a penny from me, since she was your only 'acknowledged' parent. But I've always wanted to contribute from afar. It's only fair. I don't mind that she sent you."

Duncan stared at this man who dressed like a boy and

was supposed to be his father. "I'm not here for money," he said coldly. "My mother doesn't even know I came. We have our own money."

Thriftee Mike looked surprised. "Your mother's salary isn't great," he said. "But that was the only position available at the store right now—"

"I won five thousand dollars in a Scrabble tournament," Duncan interrupted. "I plan on giving it all to her—*most* of it to her," he corrected himself, thinking of the skateboard— "though she says she won't take it. But I'm going to make sure she does."

Thriftee Mike kept gazing at him. His expression shifted very slightly. "I did know about that tournament," he said.

"You did?"

"Yes," he said. "It was on the news. 'Drilling Falls Boys Win Big.' When I saw it was you, I was . . . well, I was . . . startled." He put his hand to his face, covering his eyes, and now this boyish-looking, deeply uncomfortable man seemed upset. Duncan couldn't understand it.

"Why were you startled?" Duncan asked.

"We have something in common," Thriftee Mike said after a moment. He smiled faintly, crookedly, embarrassed. "I play a little."

"You *do*?" Duncan's mother hadn't said this, and surely she would have, had she known. Maybe she didn't know;

maybe he had taken up the game after he had left her and Duncan over twelve years earlier.

Michael Scobee nodded. "I'm not all that good. I could be a lot better. I used to play sometimes with your mother," he said. "We were so young then. She had one of those classic sets, the old-fashioned kind. It was in a maroon box. We'd play downtown at Slice's."

Duncan remembered the old score sheet that he had shown his mother. She had been the one to keep score in that long-ago game. She had written "Caroline," versus "Ms.," and she'd told Duncan that "Ms." had been her teacher, Ms. Thorp.

Duncan understood that once again, while trying to protect him, his mother hadn't told him the whole truth. "Ms." hadn't stood for "Ms. Thorp." It had been a set of initials, "MS."

Michael Scobee.

His mother had played Scrabble with his father long ago, getting a little oil from their pizza on the score sheet, before Duncan Dorfman was even born. She didn't want him to know any of this now, because she was still so angry at Michael Scobee for walking away forever, and she didn't want Duncan to think he had anything in common with this man. This man who was his father.

"I'd say we should sit down right now and play a game,"

his father said, drily. "But I have a feeling you don't want to do that."

"No," said Duncan. "I don't." Playing a game with this man was the last thing in the world he wanted to do.

"I can understand that. Perhaps sometime, anyway, you can give me some tips," said Michael Scobee. Then, bizarrely, he added, "I hate you."

"What did you say?" said Duncan. He knew his father hadn't wanted to be a father, but . . . *hate*? How could he say such a hostile thing to his son?

"I said I hate U," his father repeated, and this time Duncan heard it right. "I hate V, too," his father went on. "Those two letters always give you a lousy rack, don't you think?"

"Yes," said Duncan, his shoulders relaxing slightly. "I do."

They stood and looked at each other, continuing to size each other up. "I have to tell you," said his father, "that I never wanted it to be like this. This isn't me. Not me at all." His voice sounded choked and faraway. "Your mother is a very proud person," he went on. "After I told her I didn't think I could . . . be in your lives . . . I offered to take care of the two of you financially. She said no. I believe you that she didn't send you here tonight," he said. "But I want you to know that years ago I made a few provisions for you on my own. They're here whenever you want them."

"What's that supposed to mean, Mike?" Aunt Djuna said. "Duncan doesn't know what it means, and neither do I."

Duncan had almost forgotten that his great-aunt was standing there. For the past few minutes it had just been him and his father. Michael Scobee reached into his top desk drawer and took something out. He stretched his arm over to Duncan and nodded. At first, Duncan kept his own arm by his side. Then, reluctantly, he put out his arm and opened his fingers and felt something fall into his palm. It was a key.

"Safe-deposit box number eighty-five at the Drilling Falls Savings Bank," said his father. "Eight-five."

"Eight-five," said Duncan, thinking for a moment. "Like August fifth, my birthday."

"Exactly. When you're ready, you can go down to the bank with your mother and open it. I understand she may not approve, but you'll have to work that out with her. Maybe Djuna can help. At any rate, you are now the holder of the key."

"I don't get it," said Duncan. "You never once tried to see me all this time. You never even let me know that you still *existed*."

His father shook his head. "I don't know what to say. I've got no excuse in the world. Twelve years ago I was given a big test, and I totally failed it. And I've been failing it ever since." He paused. "But for what it's worth, and I know it's not worth much, every year on August fifth I've done a big display here in the store. All the employees prepare for weeks in advance. I have toy trains running through the place, and confetti, and a giant cake; the works. Kids love it. I've always pretended that it's the store's birthday, but that isn't true. It's yours."

For most of the drive back to the house, Duncan and his great-aunt didn't say much. It was understood that they would keep this nighttime visit to themselves. Soon enough they would tell his mother what they had done; just not yet. As they neared the house, Aunt Djuna said, "I always thought your mother should let him share some of the financial burden. I still say she should. Maybe that can happen now. Unless that safe-deposit box is like one of those big bins in his store. Filled with—"

"—flip-flops," said Duncan.

"Or spatulas," said his great-aunt.

"Or cans of jalapeño Cheezy Chips!" Duncan said, and they both laughed a little, then yawned in synchrony.

"And while she's at it," Aunt Djuna continued, "your mother ought to let you pick out your own shirts by now. I bet you'd pick different ones if you had your way; am I right? I'll bring up the subject with her, if you don't feel you can do it yourself. Also," she said, "I see that there's a new migraine pill on the market. It's called Throbbex. I

289

saw a commercial for it while I was watching you on TV, Duncan. They say it works wonders. At least the actors on the commercial say that. Maybe your mother could try it. Again, just a thought."

The banging little car pulled into the driveway of the unlit house at just past two in the morning. Duncan thanked his great-aunt and said he didn't know what he would have done without her. Once inside, he watched as she walked off to her room down the hall, moving very slowly, her shoulders stooped inside the green sweater that she had been wearing for more years than he had been alive.

Duncan put the key his father had given him into the pencil holder on his desk. It dropped in with a metallic click. It would stay there until he decided it was time to tell his mother about it. He looked around his little room before getting into bed, and he saw the certificate from the YST on the wall. For just a moment, something made him close his eyes and place the fingers of his left hand carefully over the document. He willed his so-called power to life, and immediately his fingertips warmed up to a comfortable and then an uncomfortable temperature.

Duncan read aloud, "THIS CERTIFIES THAT DUNCAN DORF..." Then the heat lowered and the words were muddied. He tried harder, but he was very sleepy, so it didn't happen as fast as usual, but it did happen. "THIS

CERTIFIES THAT DUNCAN DORFMAN HAS BEEN A PARTICIPANT IN THE YST . . ."

The sensitivity in his fingertips was still in place. Who knew where it had come from originally—whether it had been inherited, or was a quirk that had come out of nowhere. Who knew whether he and his father had more in common than the love of a word game. Other kids had other talents, too. Duncan thought of the kids he'd gotten to know in Yakamee, and how they each probably had some secret little thing about them that none of the others had. Something that made them different, quietly powerful, even if no one else knew it.

At school the following week, a girl named Emily Bean would show everyone that she could sing backward—"Any song, just try me!" she'd say—and the other kids would gather around her, the same way they had gathered around Duncan. "Row, Row, Row Your Boat," someone would call out. And she would agreeably sing, *"Wor, Wor, Wor ruoy taob . . ."*

But even though Duncan's skill, his strange and unusual power, was probably no longer of enormous interest to very many people, it was still *his*. Not that he had any plans ever to use it again, but, of course, you never knew.

First thing in the morning at school, Duncan Dorfman and Carl Slater were greeted like heroes. An assembly was held in the auditorium in their honor, and the a cappella group,

The Drilltones, sang, and the orchestra played a piece with a squeaky-clarinet solo that seemed to go on forever. Principal Gloam said, "You boys have brought glory to Drilling Falls Middle School. And for this, we honor you."

"You'd think we were astronauts," Carl whispered to Duncan out of the side of his mouth as they sat together on the stage.

Duncan and Carl weren't really friends, and they didn't have much to say to each other. They could continue to discuss their triumph, of course, but that would get boring fast. At 10:45 A.M. on his first day back, Duncan entered the school cafeteria, where the lunch-lady giantess was screaming, like always.

"PUT DOWN THAT KETCHUP RIGHT THIS MINUTE, OR I AM GOING TO CALL PRINCIPAL GLOAM!" she thundered at a girl who held a tiny ketchup packet, and who seemed bewildered that she was being screamed at because of it.

The Scrabble Club was sitting where they always sat, and today they were much friendlier than usual. They immediately made a place for Duncan, a spot where his tray would fit. At the table across the way sat Andrew Tanizaki. He didn't look at all miserable or lonely sitting by himself. He sat with his red tray in front of him, one hand pushing French fries into his mouth, the other hand holding up a new video-game booklet, which he seemed deeply absorbed in reading.

"Hey," said Duncan, walking over.

Andrew Tanizaki looked up in surprise. "Hey," he said.

Duncan sat down across from him. "Listen, thanks for everything," he said. "The good-luck drawing you gave me. And, of course, the way you covered my face up on that poster. That was amazing."

"Oh, you saw," Tanizaki said, pleased. "Which one did you see? I did it on five of them. All over town."

"Five? You *did*? I only saw the one on the bus shelter at Oakdale and Main. And I just want to say that I really, really appreciate it," Duncan said. "I mean, you have no idea how much I appreciate it."

"No problem," said Andrew Tanizaki.

Today Duncan had his backpack with him. He placed it on the bench, and then he pulled something out that had barely fit inside. It was the old maroon Scrabble set that had been in the closet. The set that his mother and father used to play on when they were very young, the set that now belonged to him.

Duncan would need a new partner if he was going to go to the YST again next year. Since he'd gotten home the day before, he'd already received three e-mails from kids at the tournament, telling him he *had* to come back. But Duncan

293

would also need a new partner just for casual games after school, or on weekends.

"You play?" he asked.

Andrew Tanizaki shook his head. "Only video games. Terra Firma and Avengicon III. Not Scrabble. Not yet."

Duncan Dorfman opened the box.

Acknowledgments

I owe a great deal to Cornelia Guest, who is known in Scrabble circles for her wisdom, kindness, and generosity. Cornelia has provided support and advice to many passionate Scrabble-playing kids and their parents, as well as to this writer, who is very grateful. My terrific older son, Gabriel, gallantly agreed to forego his beloved Clue in favor of many family games of Scrabble, and I thank him for that. (He's also a strong Scrabble player, I might add.) My husband, Richard Panek, has frequently joined in, and he has also been a great Scrabble-tournament chaperone and all-around enthusiast of anything having to do with words. My editor, Julie Strauss-Gabel, has been astute and thoughtful at every stage, and has helped make Duncan, April, and Nate who they are today; it's been a great pleasure to work with her. Don Weisberg at Penguin is an enormously encouraging and supportive presence to writers, and I am so glad to know him. My agent, Suzanne Gluck, expertly guided the way into the gratifying realm of children's books, and I thank her for this, and so much else. Finally, I owe many thanks to my parents, Hilma and Morty Wolitzer, who gave me life. Oh, and a Scrabble set.